She turned slowly in her sleeping bag to face him, her face inches from his own.

'Goodnight, Jack,' she whispered.

Before he realised what she was doing she'd leaned in towards him and touched his lips softly with hers. She smelled sweetly of the baby wipes she'd smuggled in, and she tasted of toothpaste—and the moment her lips were against his he had absolutely no chance.

Before she could move away he raised a hand and slid his fingers into her hair, tugging it from its loose tie and relishing its silkiness, his thumbs stroking along the softness of her jaw. The silk of her skin beneath his hands was delicious, the closeness tantalisingly unfamiliar in the outdoor situation. He tilted her face gently. Another kiss, his own kiss this time, deeper, a chance to savour her.

The fire spat and popped behind her. Evie was vaguely aware of it warming her back as his tongue slipped softly against her own. One of her hands crept up and around his neck, and with the other she felt her way slowly over the padded sleeping bag to curl it around his back.

Delicious heat coursed through her as she pushed her reservations aside. Jack Trent was not some wannabe partygoer, desperate for the kudos of bedding *Miss Knightsbridge*. He had his own life, his own agenda, and he wasn't remotely seduced by shallow motivations. This was not a repeat of her same old mistake, made again and again in her desperation for love and approval. He was different. With him she could be herself, and for once that was good enough.

Dear Reader

I wrote this story in the middle of winter, just after Christmas, in that lull during the New Year when going out is on the back burner and it's cold outside. I spent rather a lot of my evenings back then cozied up on the sofa in my pyjamas, fighting my husband for the remote control and watching all kinds of TV. And it was on one of those evenings that the first seeds of this story came together.

If, like me, you've ever watched a reality TV show and thought *There's no way that person is really as in-your-face as that...* or *That situation has to have been a set-up...* then you'll know exactly where I'm coming from with Evie and Jack's story. It's a story of larger-than-life alter egos and hidden backgrounds, and the world of reality TV is the perfect backdrop for it. A place where you can hide your faults or your past behind an image and be whoever you want to be. Public approval can be a hard thing to give up, but Evie and Jack must work hard to see past the TV hype if they are to find happiness.

The setting for this book was great fun to plan and write—and, as always, I hope I can entertain you!

Love

Charlotte x

MAN VS. SOCIALITE

BY
CHARLOTTE PHILLIPS

ABERDEENSHIRE LIBRARIES	
3152202	
Bertrams	29/10/2014
ROM	£13.50

First published in Great Britain 2014
by Mills & Boon, an imprint of Harlequin (UK) Limited,
Eton House, 18-24 Paradise Road, Richmond, Surrey, TW9 1SR

ISBN: 978-0-263-24332-1

Charlotte Phillips has been reading romantic fiction since her teens, and she adores upbeat stories with happy endings. Writing them for Mills & Boon® is her dream job. She combines writing with looking after her fabulous husband, two teenagers, a four-year-old and a dachshund. When something has to give, it's usually housework. She lives in Wiltshire.

Other Modern Tempted™ titles by Charlotte Phillips:

SLEEPING WITH THE SOLDIER*
THE PLUS-ONE AGREEMENT

The Flat in Notting Hill

**This and other titles by Charlotte Phillips
are also available in eBook format
from www.millsandboon.co.uk**

DEDICATION

For my mum, with love and hugs.

CHAPTER ONE

THE THING ABOUT smartphones was that when you were public enemy number one you could pick up all derogatory comments about you in one place. Convenient, *not*.

A post online...

Like to see @evieITgirl eat roasted rat. Where does she get off bad-mouthing @SurvivalJackT? #shallow

New Social Network group...

Sack Evie Staverton-Lynch from reality TV show Miss Knightsbridge. 15000 likes and counting.

Video currently going viral...

Watch It-girl Evangeline Staverton-Lynch accuse TV survival expert Jack Trent of sham expeditions.

The hit counter was heading towards six figures and the hateful mobile-phone clip had only been posted two days ago.

Crisis talks were called that for a reason. Evie turned off her phone with its tirade of abuse and sipped the horrible coffee in the office of the one person who might be able to get her out of this hole she'd dug for herself.

Chester Smith, PR to the stars, to whom she'd pledged a percentage of her income for the foreseeable future and whose manipulation of the media was responsible for her meteoric rise from insignificant socialite with too much time on her hands to darling of the reality-show-viewing public, sat on the opposite side of the glass desk. Signed glossy framed photos beamed from the office walls showing TV stars past and present whose über-successful careers had been managed by him. The desk was spread with a selection of the day's tabloids. She could see grainy stills of her own face on the front page of at least three of them. Chester tossed his perfectly styled quiff, pulled out a tablet, flipped back the gaudy cover and tapped 'play' on the mobile-phone video, as if Evie hadn't had it playing on a humiliating loop in her head for the last forty-eight hours.

There she was, picture quality not great but still perfectly unmistakeable, her favourite designer clutch on the pristine white tablecloth next to her water glass. Her father, stiff-backed, sat opposite her with his back to the camera. In the background she could see the other people lunching earlier this week at the glossy Knightsbridge eaterie, a popular celebrity hangout. And wasn't that exactly why she'd chosen that venue when her father had demanded they meet? Her father never suggested or asked when it came to seeing Evie, he *demanded*. When he said lunch, you said how many courses. And if she was going to sit through a couple of hours of criticism she might as well do it on her own territory, somewhere she'd at last begun to feel she fitted in.

She'd even had a couple of fans of the show interrupt the lunch to ask for photos. Her father's disapproval had surged towards breaking point each time—and hadn't that rather been the point? She might not be appreciated by him, might in fact be pretty much insignificant these days unless she somehow showed him up, but at least here she felt as if she was among people who liked her, even if it *was* the carefully manufactured prom-queen version of her they saw on screen.

After twenty-odd years of Evie feeling inconsequential and pointless, the public interest and support that followed her appearance in hit reality TV show *Miss Knightsbridge* had been the stuff of dreams.

Turned out it was the fickle kind of support that could be undone with one stupid wrong move.

Chester fiddled with the tablet until the clip was full-screen at maximum sound.

'No, I don't watch your show,' her father's deep clipped voice boomed out. 'I have absolutely no desire to watch you make a spectacle of yourself on national television. I find it inexplicable that the viewing public would have the slightest interest in how you spend your time.' There was a pause as her father took a sip of his white wine. She could see her own smile fold in on itself on the opposite side of the table. 'Should I happen to put the television on, I would be watching the other side. *Jack Trent's Survival Camp Extreme*.'

There was a pause in the conversation. The background buzz of the restaurant could be heard in the gap. Evie wasn't sure even now which revelation had rendered her speechless—the simple fact that her father watched television at all these days or his traitorous allegiance to the rival show in the ratings to her own.

After nigh on twenty years of trying and failing, at first to please him and eventually just to *interest* him, you'd think she would have developed the skin of a rhino by now. This last year the sudden sensation of being liked, of being *popular*, had been like a dream. After being unexpectedly scouted by the TV production company for *Miss Knightsbridge*, Evie had found that public affection had even more unexpectedly followed. Interviews and magazine photo shoots poured in as the popularity of the show climbed. And on the back of it all she was just launching her very own jewellery line, a dream she'd secretly nurtured for years but had never before had the confidence to take forward. A new business. Surely *that* would impress her father. The hoped-for happy response to the news that she would be making a living for *herself* now instead of cruising along on the cushion of her allowance was instead lost to his disapproval of the TV show. She wondered for a moment what job she would have to do to elicit his good opinion. Brain surgeon, perhaps.

'Making a spectacle of yourself for all to see,' he was saying. 'After the upbringing you've had.'

Heaven forbid that he might miss an opportunity to mention her upbringing, the implication ever-present that she should be grateful she still had one, never mind that it had been devoid of anything really except for his money and use of his name. Love and affection had been laughed out of the room from the moment her mother died, no matter how hard she tried to earn them. Her membership of the family had only ever been an honorary one, extended to her for the sake of her mother's feelings when she was alive and her mother's memory now she was dead.

'Thank goodness your mother isn't here to see it,' he added.

That last comment hit her low in the stomach and took

her breath away even when she watched it back, knowing it was coming, because perhaps the most delicious part of designing her jewellery line had been imagining the glee her mother might have felt about it. Her mum had loved costume jewellery, letting six-year-old Evie play dress-up with her box of sparkly cocktail rings and beads. The memory was a treasured one, a sparkling one among many, many later memories that were grey with obedience, routine and loneliness.

And that more than anything had triggered the thundering, ill-judged lashing-out that followed.

Now, in the cold light of a few days later, Evie's insides churned in anticipatory mortification at what came next on the tape.

Her own voice kicked in on the video, and did she really sound that pinched and snobby? Another surge of hot shame climbed her neck to burn in her face.

'Jack Trent's ex-army, isn't he?' she heard herself snap. 'So it comes as no surprise that you'd prefer watching *his* show to mine.'

She'd had her fill of military-style closing of ranks growing up. After her mother had gone she simply hadn't possessed enough female clout by herself to counteract the cold and regimented male-dominated life that was left. The new revelation that apparently a background in the armed forces ranked above his regard for her raised her temper to even dizzier heights.

'Trent's show is a documentary,' her father snapped. 'Completely different. It has substance. Five minutes of your fly-on-the-wall was enough. It's nothing but vacuous rubbish. You've turned the family into a laughing stock.'

The family. Not *our* family. Figure of speech? Or dead giveaway about how he regarded her? She seemed to see her exclusion in his every nuance these days. The difference between her and her brother Will that had never mattered when her mother was there to provide the link that held them together. *Half-brother*, she corrected now in her mind. She was the cuckoo in the nest since her mother had gone, no one left any more to justify her place there. The sadness of that thought had brought a sudden burst of irrational jealous hostility towards Jack Trent and his stupid survival skills. She gathered all the hurt and misery and frustration together and verbalised it, and unfortunately Jack Trent, whom she'd never met, happened to be inadvertently in the firing line.

'*Substance?*' she snarled. 'I can't believe you buy into all that. Do you *really* think he's sleeping under the stars eating barbecued rat? When the camera switches off he'll be off to the nearest luxury hotel to sleep on duck-down pillows and scoff à la carte.'

An audible sucking in of breath from Chester brought her right back to the horrible present.

'You know, it doesn't matter how many times I hear that, it doesn't lose its shock value,' he breathed, tapping the tablet to pause the video. A grainy freeze-frame of her own miserable and indignant expression filled the screen. Her head had started to ache.

'What were you *thinking*? You've probably ruined your own career in a couple of sentences and you've dragged Jack Trent down with you. The production company are apoplectic.'

'It was a private opinion,' she protested, the injustice of the whole thing spiking her anger. In actual fact it hadn't even *been* an opinion, it had been a lashing-out, no time to be held back by a little thing like the fact it wasn't *true*. 'Jack Trent's show just happened to be the one my father mentioned he watched instead of mine. It was a knee-jerk reaction, not meant for public viewing.'

'What you failed to consider is that the production company who make *Miss Knightsbridge* also make *Jack Trent's Survival Camp Extreme*. The tabloids are implying that means it isn't an off-the-cuff bitchy comment, that you must have some insider information.' Chester leaned in. 'That Jack Trent really *is* eating hotel food instead of living off nature's bounty.'

Not one to let up for a moment, he swiped the screen a couple of times and brought up the social network group page she'd seen earlier.

'Jack Trent's fan base are extremely loyal,' he said. '"Get evil Evie off our TV screens,"' he read aloud. 'Now sixteen thousand likes and counting—'

Unlike her fans. She had yet to read as much as a single supportive comment. A spike of miserable envy jabbed her in the stomach at the depth of public affection for Jack Trent.

She put her head in her hands and stared down at the glass table top in despair.

'Please, I don't want to hear any more.'

Now she wished she'd bitten her tongue before she'd spoken, but her subconscious mind had simply taken over in that moment of stress. Jack Trent was an ex-soldier, bound to be another cold and detached military man. He was basically her father minus thirty or so years, and so he happened to be a handy by-proxy target.

Because even after all these years of indifference at best and criticism at worst, Evie still couldn't bring herself to diss her father. Not to his face anyway.

Unfortunately she hadn't reckoned for a moment on having her comments overheard by the world at large. And apparently an immediate apology via social media just didn't cut the mustard when an inflammatory comment went viral.

'In the public consciousness right now you are pond life, sweetie.' Chester pointed at her with his pen. 'And worse than that, you're pond life with *money*. Public support has been based around fascination with your ditsy-but-sweet image, your how-the-other-half-live fashion sense and your socialite mates. That kind of thing doesn't hold much water now you've bad-mouthed a national treasure. They think they've seen the real you, and, honey, it ain't pretty.'

He tapped the screen again and shoved it in front of Evie's face. She batted the tablet aside, but unfortunately not before she'd seen the comment at the top of the list.

@evieTgirl lives in luxury. @SurvivalJackT fought for his country #wasteofspace

She clapped her hands over her eyes and pressed her palms against her eyelids. On the opposite side of the table criticism carried on. Unfortunately she didn't have enough hands to cover her ears too.

Jack Trent gritted his teeth and climbed out of the taxi at the glossy offices of Purple Productions, the usual sense of resignation kicking in at time required to be spent schmoozing in the city, which he considered to be time completely wasted. He wondered if he would ever in his life get the train into London without then counting the hours until he could get the train back out again.

Back in the wilderness at the outward-bound centre he owned in the Scottish Highlands, fine-tuning preparations were unexpectedly on hold for his latest venture, one which for the first time meant more than just a business opportunity based on his military skills. This new initiative was close to his heart. He had more invested in it than just time and money. The sudden requirement to leave and come to talk to suits would have had his mood on a knife edge at the best of times, let alone when he was on the cusp of such an important new venture.

Yet he came all the same, because the publicity he'd gained since his adventures had been televised had given him clout that was worth something. His survival-course business had skyrocketed. A meeting here, a party or a photo opportunity there, and now he was at a point where he could kick his actions up to another level, beyond just fund-raising. His carefully devised courses for kids were on the brink of being a reality, a way at last to make a real difference that might compensate for his past mistakes. He hadn't needed to come to the city that often to keep his agent happy and his popularity high. And with the launch of this new course he needed that popularity more than ever.

The unexpected revelation that the Internet was awash with a rumour that his notoriously tough survival-skills documentaries were actually bullshit was so unbelievable that at first he thought it was a joke. Surfing the Internet wasn't at the top of his priority list at any time, certainly not when he was in the middle of nowhere risk-assessing potential sites for river crossings. As a result the rumour was at full pelt in the media before he knew a thing about it. A phone call from one of his employees informing him that he was currently trending online confirmed that, no, unfortunately, it was perfectly true. He'd watched the offending video and he'd had plenty of time on the train to read about the backlash in the press, invariably accompanied by an endless collection of glamour shots of Evangeline Staverton-Lynch.

By the time he reached London he had all the sorry details and if the situation wasn't rectified to his satisfaction, heads would roll. No matter how pretty they might be.

Evie got into the car next to Chester the following morning with her head held high, hair and make-up perfect, her pink designer suit carefully chosen because it was the furthest thing in her wardrobe from demure black. She'd had plenty of time to get her frame of mind right because she'd barely slept, not that anyone else needed to know that. She'd grimly painted out the dark shadows under her eyes with concealer and added a slick of pink lip gloss. Ready to channel defiance, because in her experience contrite got you nowhere.

The part of her that hadn't slept wanted to grovel apologies at Jack Trent and then hide in her little flat in Chelsea for possibly the rest of her life. She refused obstinately to listen to that Evie. That Evie was the same one who even after twenty years still wanted her mum, who'd ached to go home when she was dropped at boarding school and who'd tried everything she could think of to secure her father's good opinion. Instead, his particular blend of parental indifference had spiralled down the years into disapproval until the only thing that seemed to spike his interest was a climbing scale of outrageous or shocking behaviour. And so that was what she'd delivered. In spades.

After finding that he wouldn't bother turning up at school for shows or open days but would descend on the place in full and scary military uniform when she was reprimanded for smoking and for dancing on the tables during prep, a brand-new Evie had come to the fore. This new incarnation was a master at I-don't-care. And she'd had her feet under the table for so long now that the Evie who felt mortified and guilt-ridden at the grief she'd caused Jack Trent most certainly wasn't about to surface and take the flak.

It was a beautiful spring morning, cold but sunny. Perfect for a spot of shopping in South West London and then maybe coffee at a pavement café. Chance would be a fine thing. The way things were right now any beverage drunk in public might very well be tipped over her head by an indignant pensioner. Jack Trent's supporters were everywhere and age was no boundary.

'We're meeting the executive producer of *Miss Knightsbridge* and some of the production team,' Chester briefed her as the car nosed its way through the London morning traffic. 'They want to talk through the situation, explore some options.'

'You mean they want to sack me.'

His lack of reply didn't instil confidence.

She followed Chester through the glossy reception of Purple Productions, its walls festooned with glossy stills from its string of über-successful shows. Behind the reception desk she saw a shot taken from *Miss Knightsbridge* of herself walking down Brompton Road with armfuls of designer carrier bags. Unfortunately a few rows along her eyes fell on a photo of Jack Trent, up to his neck in hideous river water as he manoeuvred his way with a machete through dense reeds and river debris. His face was smeared with mud. Her stomach gave a nervous churn.

She could feel the disapproving eyes of the rubbernecking office staff boring into her as she walked. It felt as if she were about to be lynched. Right now she wished she'd bitten off her own tongue before she'd spoken so recklessly.

It was immediately obvious on entering the board-room why the typing pool had been looking at her as if she were an interesting new species of worm. Jack Trent was leaning back in his chair on the opposite side of the meeting table with an expression on his face that implied he'd quite like to see her head on a spike. Her stomach plummeted like a stone. The photo in Reception and the glimpses she'd caught of him on TV or in the odd magazine hadn't done him justice. He had the broadest chest of any man she'd ever seen, solid muscle beneath the tailored shoulders of his dark jacket. His light brown hair was very short, not much more than military buzz cut, and his face sported a small scar high on the left chiselled cheekbone and a tan the depth of which could only be achieved from spending days on end outdoors without wearing anything so namby-pamby as sunblock. He met her gaze with green eyes that might have been stomach-melting if they hadn't been furious. He was without a shred of doubt gorgeous eye candy of the highest order. If you liked the cold-hearted, detached, wants-to-kill-you soldier look, that was.

She didn't.

Also around the table she recognised members of the *Miss Knightsbridge* production team. Hostility radiated from them and she curled her hands into damp fists at her sides and averted her eyes from the antagonistic ex-pressions. She'd made a stupid smartass comment; she'd never meant it to be repeated publicly; it was a mistake, nothing more. She did *not* deserve to be hung out to dry. She gritted her teeth, determined not to give away that she was upset. She would brazen it out, exactly the way she always did. Defiant brave face, that was the thing. Tried and tested, relied on throughout her life.

Even so, humiliation bubbled hotly upward from her

neck and and boiled in her cheeks as she took a chair as close to the door as possible, in case the brave-face thing didn't work and the suppressed urge to bolt and just hide for the next ten years in her flat in Chelsea got the better of her.

Jack Trent watched Evie walk into the boardroom with her perfectly coiffed head held high. She wore her hair loose, its glossy waves threaded with perfect tones of toffee and gold that looked deliciously touchable but which surely depended on endless wasted hours in a top salon. Her eyes were wide and baby blue, there was a tiny spray of freckles on her nose, and her mouth with its deliciously full lower lip was painted pale pink. She was the perfect example of English rose. She was tall and slender in the beautifully cut pink suit with short skirt and his mind insisted on treating him to a delectable flash of the photos he'd seen of her in the press on the way here, wearing a silk slip and a very cute smile.

He looked away, not without some difficulty, and refocused his mind carefully on the unbelievable mess she'd single-handedly made of his reputation with a couple of sentences.

'Jack, this is Evangeline Staverton-Lynch,' the company PR said at his elbow.

He took a breath and met her gaze across the table. She held his eyes with her own clear blue defiant ones, and if he'd been expecting a grovelling apology he'd apparently be waiting a long time. Clearly she was just another vacuous self-obsessed TV wannabe—only interested in her own fame and fortune. He knew the type only too well.

She nodded at him from across the table and beamed a perfect smile as if she hadn't thrown the survival of his pet project into the balance. Four years ago this month since he'd left the army, and it had taken this long to reach a point where he could maybe begin to siphon off some of the guilt at what had happened while he'd been away. He'd believed enlisting would be the answer to all his problems, and it had been. His own slate wiped clean, a fresh start for him. The payoff had been the life left behind for his mother and sister and the nightmare Helen had drifted into without him there to look out for her. Too late now to change the past for Helen, but his work could still make a difference to others like her. He'd put his heart and soul into it and now, thanks to this diva, it looked as if the whole thing was going to fail before it even got off the ground.

'I should be in Scotland right now,' he snapped before anyone else could speak. 'Working on the final kit list for my kids' twenty-four-hour survival-skills course. It's meant to be piloting in schools next month. I've been working towards this for the past two years, it's the sole reason I've kept up the TV shows, and now I find the whole thing is hanging by a thread because of some libellous comment made by *you*. You don't even know me.'

Evie straightened her back and pressed her teeth together to keep the not-my-fault smile in place. It would have been so much easier somehow if his TV show were the limit of his remit. A small twist of envy knotted her stomach at the thought of his survival business, at his drive and direction in life. The Jack Trent that existed outside the TV screen clearly had a lot more substance than Evie Staverton-Lynch did when you stripped away her own media image.

She resorted to the method that had dug her out of many a scrape throughout school: do not admit responsibility. And followed it up by pasting on a smile and mustering up as much charm as she could manage.

She leaned forward in her chair and offered him a demure smile.

'Look, Jack—can I call you Jack?'

He stared at her incredulous but she carried on regardless.

'This has all been a *vile* misunderstanding. It was a private comment, taken completely out of context. Filmed without my knowledge or consent. Honestly, these people have no respect for anyone's privacy. But please don't worry.' She sat back and nodded reassuringly as if she had the whole ridiculous debacle under some level of control. In her dreams. 'I issued an immediate retraction via social media.'

'Are you having some kind of a laugh?' he shouted. 'A retraction via social media? Too little, too bloody late.' He held her gaze angrily until she finally dropped her eyes. 'Half the country have heard you bad-mouthing me. The papers are full of it. Mud like that sticks.'

She pushed her hands into her hair and stared down at the table.

'I'm *truly sorry* for any inconvenience this has caused you but I can't be responsible for something filmed without my knowledge. It wasn't directed at you. I was having an argument with my father and I spoke without thinking. If I could take it back I would. If there's anything I can do to fix the situation, I will.'

She smiled winningly at him. He scowled back.

'Delighted to hear you say that, because we have a solution.' The executive producer at the head of the table interrupted and held her hands up for silence. '*Miss Knightsbridge* and *Survival Camp Extreme* are, as you know, both made by Purple Productions. Very different, admittedly, but both are under our control. As such, this is why the current media backlash is so damaging. The tabloids have been quick to notice the connection and it lends credence to the accusations made against Jack.'

Evie felt Jack's eyes on her again and she forced herself to look right back at him. The green eyes didn't flicker as he stared her down. Her charm offensive didn't seem to be having much of an effect. What the hell else could she do? This whole damn thing had been blown out of all proportion.

'These are our two top-rated shows and without some intervention there's likely to be a knock-on effect on the ratings of both.' The producer took a breath. 'Fortunately we've been able to come up with a suggestion that will harness this backlash and turn it into something positive.'

'Harness it?' Jack said. His voice was strong and deep. Indeterminable accent—no clipped Britishness like her father. She caught herself wondering vaguely what his background was, where he was from.

'There's no such thing as bad publicity, Jack. Remember that.' Chester, the only person in her camp and he was paid to be there, pointed his pen at Jack's angry face from his seat next to Evie.

'There is when it undermines everything I've worked for,' he growled.

'What we're proposing is a one-off special.' The producer spoke over them and then paused for effect. '*Miss Knightsbridge Meets Survival Camp Extreme.*'

There was a stunned silence around the table.

CHAPTER TWO

'ARE YOU SAYING what I think you're saying?' Evie's stomach felt suddenly as if a brick had been dumped inside it. She had absolutely no desire to spend even a single second more in the company of Jack Trent. And from the way he was looking at her it was clear the feeling was mutual.

The producer clapped her hands together excitedly.

'Absolutely. You guest on Jack's show. One of his usual survival quests. It's not such an off-the-wall suggestion—he's had guests on before, demonstrating survival techniques, sampling bush tucker, that kind of thing. A day or two with the bare essentials, during which you experience Jack's survival skills at first hand. It will take advantage of the massive public interest and makes it work to our advantage. Think about it. Could there *be* a better retraction than that?'

She beamed an encouraging smile in Evie's direction. 'You know the kind of thing. I'm thinking you serve up some kind of foraged meal and sleep in a shelter made of sticks you've built yourself. Perhaps do a river crossing. The public will lap it up. You can eat your words on national TV, you restore Jack's reputation and hopefully we boost the ratings of both shows in the process. Really, it's genius.'

'No way!'

Evie was on her feet to protest, beaten by a split second by Jack Trent on the opposite side of the boardroom table. He was a good foot taller than her, a dark green shirt beneath his jacket picking out the darker tones in his eyes, and he certainly commanded attention. The eyes of everyone around the table, including her own, swivelled in his direction. Even his choice of daywear came from a camouflage colour palette. Shock-horror. For the first and possibly the last time, he agreed with her.

'You're not messing with the *Survival Camp* format,' Jack said shortly. 'This ridiculous charade has nothing to do with me. Reprimand the socialite princess if you want to, drop her show, sue her for damages, I really don't care. I'm not the one who's done anything wrong here.'

Socialite princess? How *dared* he?

'Excuse me?' she snapped at him indignantly.

'Legal action *is* a possibility,' the PR manager sitting on Jack's right said.

Cold tendrils of dread thundered into Evie's heart. She glanced sideways at Chester in a panic, her mouth paper-dry as the implications of that raced through her mind. Chester had turned an interesting shade of grey, undoubtedly thinking of his own commission. They could probably take her to the cleaners over this. Jack probably could too, if the mood took him. Months of tabloid coverage yawned terrifyingly ahead of her. Her reputation and her new jewellery business would be in tatters. The thought of her father's reaction made her feel sick.

'Although it's not necessarily the best option,' the PR continued.

A tentative surge of relief kicked in because although it was clear from this that there *was* another option, it clearly wasn't going to be pleasant.

'Doesn't really matter who's wrong or right.' The executive producer took over again at the head of the table. 'I don't care and the viewing public don't give a toss either. The only thing that's important is that putting the two of you together right now is TV gold. The public are siding with Jack right now but the tabloids are still sowing that nugget of doubt. The tide could turn at any moment.' She looked directly at Jack. 'Mud really does stick. Doesn't matter that there's not an ounce of truth in it, it's been repeated so much now in so many places that public belief in the credibility of your skills is bound to be called into question. The best way to refute this is to take it and run with it. *On screen.*'

'*Survival Camp* is a serious premise,' Jack said. 'Not some reality-show fluff. It has a serious message behind it. *Look at her.*' He waved an incredulous hand in Evie's direction. 'She wouldn't last five minutes. Absolutely no way.'

The instant dismissal fired up a surge of defiance in her belly.

'I'm as fit as you are,' she snapped at him.

He laughed out loud and indignant anger burned in her cheeks, undoubtedly clashing horribly with her pink designer suit.

'You really think a few yoga classes can give you the stamina to cross a river unaided, sweetheart?' he shot back.

'I don't think you understand,' the producer cut in. 'You're both under contract to do more shows. We're within our rights to change the format as we see fit—just take a peek at the small print. Plus Adventure Bars are making noises about withdrawing sponsorship of Jack's show. I've managed to talk them round on the strength of the potential publicity of this joint show. I don't think either of you realise what a mess this is.'

'Adventure Bars?' Evie said.

The producer flapped a hand at her.

'Nutritional snack bars for hardcore outdoor types. They sponsor Jack's show. They are also,' she added in a pointed aside to Jack, 'sponsoring that spin-off outdoor activities initiative you're hoping to roll out in schools. You really think that's going to get off the ground if your main sponsor pulls out and you can't restore public confidence?'

The injustice of it all made anger sear through Jack's veins. He had to admit that the revelation that his sponsors were getting cold feet was news to him. He dug nails into his palms.

He'd piloted an outdoor survival course aimed specifically at kids and the interest had blown him away. He knew better than anyone about what a difference something like this could make to a generation of bored couch-potato kids who were either hanging around street corners waiting to be sucked into crime or were hooked on TV and video games. His sister Helen crossed his mind, never far away. If he could divert one kid from the path she'd taken, all the hard graft would be worth it. But no matter how hard he worked, taking it to the next step depended on consumer confidence and investment. Thanks to Princess Knightsbridge over there, both those things now hung in the balance and he was prepared to do anything to pull that situation back.

He realised with a burst of fury that he would have to do the one-off show. It could be the only way to make sure he obliterated all doubts about his integrity. And if she thought he'd be giving her an easy ride she was deluded.

The executive producer looked at Evie.

'Without this show, Evie, I'm afraid renewing your contract for *Miss Knightsbridge* will be out of the question. Without the joint show we'd have to find alternative ways to minimise the bad publicity. The best course of action would probably be to quietly write you out. Of course we'd have to find a new central character for the show—'

'I'll do it,' Evie cut in immediately. What choice did she have? Without this show her public image was worth nothing. There would be no more magazine articles, no more talking-heads fashion slots on daytime TV. Her fledgling jewellery business would fail before it even began. She'd be back to the quiet life, cruising along alone with no aim or direction, and this time the quiet life would probably come with hate mail. 'I'll do the foraging and the sleeping outside and the rubbing sticks together to make fire.' As an afterthought she added, 'I'd prefer not to do water though.'

Jack laughed out loud mirthlessly.

'You think you can get through an outward-bound weekend without getting wet, sweetheart? You obviously haven't watched the show. Think again.'

Of course she hadn't watched the show—was he insane? She didn't do the great outdoors. The nearest she'd ever got to it were camping holidays as a small child, and they'd never happened again after her mother died. As her *Miss Knightsbridge* image demanded, she did luxury hotels, spa treatments and shopping. On her own time she did comfy pyjamas, tea and toast, and American TV show box sets. Not a foraged meal in sight in either her public or private persona.

He was already up, striding towards the exit, his entire demeanour exuding white-hot anger. So all she had to do to regain public affection, keep her TV show and stop her fledgling jewellery business from going under was survive a weekend in rough terrain with a companion who hated her guts.

Just bloody *great*.

'You're going on a TV show with Evie Staverton-Lynch?' Helen's voice on the phone practically bubbled with interest. 'Miss Knightsbridge?'

'Unfortunately.'

'Oh, I just love her! Her clothes are to die for. Can you ask her where she got that butterfly necklace she wore on last week's show?'

Jack drew in an exasperated breath. All the girl did was wear designer clothes and hang out in swanky bars. And now it seemed his own sister was as sucked in by all the TV crap as everyone else.

'She's a reality TV star,' he pointed out. Someone had to. 'It doesn't require a modicum of talent. *Why* is she so popular? What is it about her?'

'It's the whole different world thing, isn't it? The way the other half live, the money they spend. It's cult viewing. Everyone watches it and everyone has an opinion on it. Don't you know that?'

Helen's tone had a hint of you're-too-decrepit-to-understand. The eight years between them yawned canyon-wide.

'Evie Staverton-Lynch is really cool and funny,' she added.

'Did you not see the trouble she's caused me?' he said.

Helen made a vague dismissive noise as if she was distracted. He could just imagine her watching TV while she talked to him. Multitasking, splitting her attention down the middle. A fond smile touched his lips. He loved her in-your-face attitude. It hadn't been long enough since she'd been holed up in the hospital, too weak to speak. And then there had been rehab. Would it ever be long enough?

'It's all just a publicity stunt,' she said. 'All designed to get more attention. Probably staged.'

'I need it like a hole in the head,' he said.

'You need to lighten up', she said. 'With any luck you might even come out of this looking a bit hip. Your shows have been looking a bit nerdy recently.'

He could hear the teasing smile in her voice.

'Nerdy?' A grin spread across his face at her cheek. He could never hear enough of that.

'This could get you a whole new audience.'

'Will you be watching?'

Her voice softened.

'I always watch.'

'And you're feeling OK and your college course is going fine?' he checked.

'For the hundredth time, will you stop fussing? I'm perfectly fine, I promise.'

He restrained himself from picking endlessly at her. There was a constant need to be certain she was on track, doing fine, clean. It had barely diminished since that first shocking sight of her at rock bottom, a journey she'd taken while he'd been on the other side of the world, oblivious, revelling in his army career.

'I'll call you as soon as I get back from filming,' he said.

'Evie Staverton-Lynch has the best fashion sense in the country. She'll soon have you out of that camo green you keep wearing. Good luck!' She blew him a kiss and put the phone down.

For Pete's sake.

'You don't have to go through with this.'

Annabel Sutton leaned back against the plump pink cushions on Evie's sofa and as usual said exactly what Evie wanted to hear. Annabel pulled a face as she sipped her coffee. Not her usual table in her favourite Chelsea café and clearly Evie wasn't up to supplying the usual standard of beverage. After the reaction Evie had got in the street this morning when she'd nipped to the corner shop to buy milk, she'd insisted Annabel come to her flat instead of going out. An irate pensioner had informed her that she ought to be ashamed of herself, saying those awful things about that 'nice young man'.

'None of this is your fault,' Annabel soothed. 'Total overreaction by the TV company—the whole thing's been blown out of proportion. And it's not like you're on the breadline, sweetie. You've got a whopping great allowance, this lovely flat, a country estate. You don't *need* to take this.' She paused. 'The production company *really* suggested cutting you from the show, did you say?' She gazed up at the ceiling. 'How awful. I wouldn't blame you if you walked away after that lack of support. I guess they'll move one of the rest of us into the central role.'

Secondary player on *Miss Knightsbridge*, Annabel had a part-time PR job in a glossy art gallery and a fabulously supportive family who were distantly related to the Queen. It occurred to Evie that Annabel was seeing this a bit too much like an opportunity to really pull off supportive.

'The threat of legal action was bandied about,' Evie

said shortly. 'For potential loss of income relating to Jack Trent's TV series, his business interests…I do this show, I avert the possibility of that.'

That would make sense to Annabel. A reason that was related to finance. Evie didn't mention that the money was the least of her worries. The thing that really ached the most was the loss of support, the way the public had turned on her after making her feel special for once. What she really wanted, if she was honest, was to find a way to turn that around, to get things back to the way they were. To launch her jewellery business to rapturous reviews, perhaps secure a concession in one of the department stores, instead of sinking out of sight under a cloud of public dislike.

'Plus I might be able to turn off the Internet but I still can't leave the flat without grief from the public.'

'Since when have you given a damn what other people think?'

Annabel was familiar with Evie's perfected I-don't-care-bring-on-the-fun persona. At school Evie had quickly learned that attitude earned friendship from the most popular girls. In South West London she'd continued to work at being one of the crowd, the need to belong somewhere as important to her as ever. She wasn't sure what her friends, or the TV viewers for that matter, would make of her if they knew that given the choice of falling out of a glossy nightclub and curling up with a box set, the TV show would win every time.

'Since I can't put my head outside the door without pensioners accosting me.' She thought back to this morning's encounter. It seemed age was no barrier to the charm Jack Trent held over the opposite sex.

'And you're sure Jack Trent isn't the real reason you're up for this?' Annabel said slyly. 'I mean, did you *see* him shirtless in the papers? Utterly jaw-dropping and totally eligible. He's never photographed with the same woman twice. I can think of people I'd rather kick out of the tent.'

Evie suppressed a flash of interest in scanning the tabloids online. Never the same woman twice? Familiar alarm bells clanged madly in her head. She'd fallen for looks and charm once too often only to find the person they were actually interested in bedding was TV's *Miss Knightsbridge*, along with her glossy life. Once they'd reached that base, interest in the real Evie seemed to disappear like smoke, with the possible exception of one D-list pop star she'd dated who'd spun out the charade a bit longer because he wanted a spot on the TV show. She had absolutely no interest in spending time with Jack Trent beyond salvaging her own reputation. What he looked like without a shirt and his marital status had no place in the debate.

'According to what I've read about his survival courses, I'll be lucky to even *get* a tent,' she said.

The evening before filming started and Jack arrived at the Scottish hotel habitually used by the production crew when making his TV series, and presumably the hotel Evie Staverton-Lynch had referred to in her libellous comment.

He took a small amount of pleasure in the knowledge that it was a two-star basic place, chosen because of its convenient proximity to his outward-bound centre and definitely *not* for its accommodation standards. No duck-down pillows and absolutely no gourmet menu. Fiercely defensive of their TV star guest, they'd given Evie the room above the kitchens with the view of the bins and an aroma of chip fat should she make the mistake of opening the windows.

The rest of the crew were predictably holed up in the hotel bar as per usual. There was no sign of Miss Knightsbridge anywhere although he'd expected her to descend on the place with a trail of staff behind her. He ordered a soft drink and flipped through the day's newspapers lying in a pile to one side of the bar, the front pages of nearly all the red tops featuring some gleeful article about the up-and-coming show. The production company would be made up at the media interest.

He turned a page and choked on his mineral water.

Evie Staverton-Lynch's PR team had clearly been working overtime. A double-page spread featured a colour photo of Evie looking clear-eyed at the camera and wearing a forest-green *Jack Trent's Survival Camp Extreme* T-shirt and what looked like nothing else. She had the longest, most delectable legs he'd ever seen. His mouth leached of all moisture and he took an exasperated slug of his drink. He had no wish to find her so *hot* and it might help if he didn't keep inadvertently coming across full-colour photos of her in varying delicious states of undress. He forced his eyes to the accompanying article instead. The interview hit just the right tone of contrite. *'I made a stupid untrue comment in a moment of stress. Taking the survival course is payback for that. I hope it will show how sorry I am and that Jack Trent's show is the genuine article.'*

Since when had denial of all responsibility gone out of the window in favour of doing all she could to restore his good name? He allowed himself a last look at the shapely legs and peach-glossed pout before he closed the paper. Genuine remorse or media spin? He had his doubts. He knew from past experience that people like

Evie Staverton-Lynch played the press to their own advantage, changing their attitude at a moment's notice to suit themselves. Not that he should care one bit either way as long as his reputation came out of this without a smear.

To his enormous surprise, when he checked with Reception for her room number, she hadn't made any complaint about the sparse facilities. He got the impression from the over-attentive Reception staff that the lack of diva uproar was something of a disappointment.

'She just arrived on her own, checked in and took herself up to the room. Didn't even ask for the concierge to take her bags,' the over-attentive receptionist, who according to the pink badge strategically placed on her low-cut blouse was called Sally, said. 'Haven't heard a peep from her since except for a call to Room Service.'

The staff had clearly been expecting her to storm back down as soon as she saw the room and felt cheated at the lack of bratty behaviour. For the first time he found himself wondering just how much of the spoilt socialite impression Evie gave was genuine. Small contradictions at first, lack of diva complaints about the crappy facilities when there was no camera around to witness the tantrum. The fact that she'd travelled up here completely alone. Where were the rich family and glossy friends and hangers-on?

He knew about using a public image to your advantage, despite the fact it made him feel uncomfortable. The media spotlight had done wonders for his charity work and his survival business. When in London he had a shortlist of on-off girlfriends to provide him with the perfect date when he needed to attend anything public. Models or starlets who shared the same showbusiness agent as him and were more than happy with the exposure of being seen out with him at charity functions or parties. He kept things casual at all costs. Enjoy the moment then move on; that was the way he liked it.

The tabloid press gleefully wrote about his glamorous girlfriends and his daredevil outdoor exploits and largely ignored his family background. And as a result the public at large had no clue about his youth, his past failures or about the selfish way he'd let his sister down. That was the way he intended to keep it.

Evie Staverton-Lynch's success was based entirely on manipulation of the media. That didn't necessarily mean there wasn't more to her than the papers gave away.

The hotel lift wasn't working so he took the stairs.

Expecting Room Service with what was bound to be a substandard lasagne, Evie jumped a little in surprise when she opened the door to see Jack Trent leaning laconically against the door jamb.

'What, no entourage?' he said. The green eyes held a hint of amusement, which crinkled them at the corners and made her stomach give an extremely ill-judged flutter. For Pete's sake, she was *not* attracted to a man who was going to take pleasure in making her crawl through mud this time tomorrow.

She kept hold of the door.

'Excuse me?' she said.

'Don't people like you have a gang of hangers-on that accompany you everywhere? You know, for hair and make-up and general love-ins.'

Did he have any idea of the ludicrousness of that comment? None of her friends were prepared to desert their luxury London lives for somewhere as devoid of consumer durables as this in order to offer her some support. In fact, there'd been a marked drop in contact from her social circle in these last few days. Supportive friendship apparently didn't hold much weight in the face of disassociating yourself from the bad-mouthing Jack Trent media scandal. On her own, therefore, in the middle of nowhere, she'd spent the past hour flicking through the laminated 'Hotel Information' brochure, working out that with no satellite TV the choice of movie that evening was reduced to one—a sci-fi blood-fest, just bloody *great*—and wondering if she could bear the alternative: watching something else on the tiny screen of her phone via the somewhat erratic Wi-Fi.

'*Love-ins?*' she snapped. 'Have you not been following the media? The entire country wants to see me fall flat on my face. Ideally in a swamp.'

The public interest showed no sign of abating, much to the glee of Purple Productions. Any hope that the furore might die down had long since disappeared. Her only hope, according to Chester, was to play the apology card for all she was worth, take the flak, and hope the tide would turn in her favour.

'That could be arranged,' he said.

She looked up to see a grin touch the corner of his mouth. It wasn't entirely unfriendly. It occurred to her that getting him onside could make this whole hideous situation a million times easier so she offered him a smile in return.

'Did you want something?'

'I thought I'd run through the kit list with you, check you're ready for tomorrow. I like to check in with all the candidates for my courses the night before, answer any questions, that kind of thing.'

'Very professional,' she said.

He waited, eyebrows raised, until she pushed the

door back and let him step past her into the horrible hotel room.

One of the narrow twin beds was piled high with kit delivered by an enthusiastic production minion who was clearly beside herself with glee at the prospect of Evie Staverton-Lynch freezing her arse off for the weekend in the most repellent, unglamorous set of garments she'd ever come across. She tried to imagine a single situation prior to today when she might have considered wearing waterproofs and failed to come up with one. She was a city girl; she hadn't been near the great outdoors since the childhood camping holidays her mother had loved, and they were long gone. Her father's strategy for moving on from the past had involved avoiding nostalgia trips of any kind. A new family holiday destination was quickly slotted in with the purchase of a house in France, to which she and Will were despatched a few times a year, always with a nanny. Revisiting the idea of outdoor living held an undertow of uneasiness at what memories it might dredge up.

Then again, *Survival Camp Extreme* was about as far as it was possible to get from the glimpses of sunny camping holidays by the beach that she remembered. When it came to this weekend, nostalgia was surely the least of her worries.

The minuscule room seemed infinitely smaller with Jack Trent in it and her stomach gave a traitorous flip of nerves, which she steadfastly ignored. She could schmooze with the best of them and surely even Jack Trent could be charmed. It was just a matter of hitting the right approach. She crossed the sticky carpet to the teetering pile of kit and began sifting through it, although she'd already looked through it once with growing disquiet. A balaclava lay on the top of the pile, for goodness' sake.

She could feel his eyes on her.

'All ready for tomorrow, then?' he said.

She glanced up at him. The green eyes watched her steadily and she got the oddest feeling that he knew perfectly well how she was feeling. This close she was struck by the pure muscular size of him. The plain green T-shirt moulded to his huge shoulders and broad chest. She could see part of an eagle tattoo on the rock-hard muscle of his left upper bicep.

She slapped on the don't-care smile that she'd perfected over a number of years.

'As I'll ever be,' she breezed.

'Nervous?' he pressed. She gave away the answer in the drop of her eyes and she could have kicked herself.

'It will be fine,' he said, his voice softened a little. Her stomach gave a skip in response. She hadn't really thought Jack Trent did anything as sappy as *reassurance*. 'Tough but fun, right?'

Fun?

'How the hell did you get involved in this kind of thing?' she blurted before she could stop herself. 'I mean, it's not exactly something vocational you decide on doing at school, is it? How do you come to the conclusion that the career for you will involve eating rodents and crossing freezing rivers?'

He grinned at the sudden outburst.

'Says the girl who's famous for…well, for being famous. How do you get involved in *that*?'

Her hand betrayed her and ran itself nervously through her hair before she brought it back to clench at her side.

'I am *not* remotely nervous,' she said, avoiding the

question. 'I work out five times a week, I run and I do toning with weights. I think I can manage what's basically a revved-up camping trip.'

He laughed out loud, a rich, deep sound that made her traitorous stomach go soft.

'Revved-up camping trip? Have you actually taken the time to watch any of the shows?'

'I've seen a few clips,' she said.

She wasn't about to admit to him that his shows looked like a mud-soaked freezing nightmare. No way was she just going to *take* his arrogant implication that she wasn't up to the challenge.

'Fitness is only a small part of it,' he countered. 'It's about initiative, it's about self-control, it's about how you react in a difficult situation with limited resources.' He was watching her intently as if trying to read her mind. 'I read your change of tack in the press,' he said.

'Change of tack?'

'From washing your hands of all responsibility to holding your hands up and begging for forgiveness.' He paused. 'With accompanying photo spread.'

His green eyes held hers intently without the slightest flicker and her pulse jumped at his pointed tone. She knew perfectly well which photo spread he was referring to. She swallowed to clear her suddenly dry throat. She was determined to keep control of this situation, to squash any stupid misplaced attraction to him.

'Are you complaining that I've said I'm publicly sorry?' she said.

'No, I'm just wondering whether it's genuine or just a new spin.'

She glanced up at him, the blue eyes giving nothing away.

'If it cleans any smears from your reputation, what do you care which it is?' she asked.

He shrugged.

'I don't. Not really. Just trying to get the measure of you.'

Jack watched as she abandoned the pile of kit, as if she'd had any interest in it anyway, and turned to face him, giving him her full attention. She was close enough now for him to pick up the scent of her perfume. She smelled delicious and expensive. She watched him steadily with wide blue eyes that sparked off a slow burn low in his abdomen. She was seriously cute.

'I'd really like it if we could put any bad feeling behind us,' she said. 'I know the situation is difficult but I really *am* doing all I can to put it right. I think we could both focus on the weekend ahead a lot more effectively if we made some kind of truce.'

If she thought she'd be able to charm him into going easy on her by suggesting he might not be totally focused, she was way wrong.

'How I feel about you has no effect whatsoever on my responsibility to you in the field,' he said. 'I'm a professional. Your safety is my priority.'

'So a truce isn't out of the question, then?' she pressed.

'Depends on the terms,' he said, just to see what she would do next. She was clearly used to getting her own way.

He saw her eyes widen briefly in surprise. She obviously hadn't expected him to give in so easily. She rushed on quickly while the going was good.

'Thing is, Jack,' she said, 'we both want the same thing.'

'Which is?'

She shrugged.

'To get through this weekend without any hitches,' she said. 'I know perfectly well the public want to see me slip up but would that really *be* the best showcase for your survival courses? Isn't the whole *point* that the candidates survive? With that in mind, maybe it might be…prudent…for *both* of us to approach the tasks in a way that shows the situation in the best light.'

That showed *her* in the best light, in other words. Oh, she really was something else. Her we're-on-the-same-side-here persuasion might work on other people but he'd had enough dealings with TV luvvies to develop immunity to that kind of manipulation. Fame and fortune mattered only inasmuch as they furthered what he considered to be his real work: his charity initiatives and the courses he'd developed for kids.

She smiled winningly at him and he wondered vaguely if she'd ever encountered a situation in her cushy existence without an expectation that she would somehow come out on top no matter what. Charm held no weight with him when held up against hard graft. And looking at her soft, beautifully manicured hands, he doubted there'd been much of that in her life. She was from a totally different world.

She held his gaze with wide blue eyes, waiting for him to just fling himself at her designer-clad feet and agree to her every whim.

'I think we understand each other,' he said.

'Good.' She smiled at him. He smiled broadly back at her.

'Despite your brushing it off as a—what was it?— "revved-up camping trip",' he said, 'you still want me to go easy on you this weekend. Sorry, sweetheart, the clue's in the name. It's a *survival* course, it's not meant to be a piece of cake.'

She stared at him as he headed for the door.

'I thought you came up here to check through any concerns I might have,' she said.

'I did. I meant legitimate ones, like your swimming ability or maybe questions about the kit. Not schmoozy concerns about getting an easy ride. No can do. I'll see you at the base at dawn.'

He closed the door behind him and smiled at the plastic number plate on the door. He'd give it until lunchtime tomorrow before she walked off set.

CHAPTER THREE

'So we start at Jack's base camp with him talking through the kit you need. Then you head out with him into the wilderness on foot.'

Evie clutched desperately at the sides of the passenger seat as a production assistant dressed in head to toe waterproofs bumped the Jeep along what barely passed for a muddy track. The silver-grey tendrils of dawn were creeping in across the Scottish Highlands and the landscape was soaked by a relentless drizzle of fine rain, the kind that lulled you into thinking it was nothing while insidiously soaking you to the bone. Leaving the awful hotel in the small hours had felt like leaving civilisation.

'There's a support team though—right?' she said. 'I mean, he doesn't film *himself* doing all this stuff, does he? It wouldn't just be the two of us with no backup.'

She'd made time for a bit more research after last night's encounter, courtesy of the hotel's erratic Wi-Fi. Footage of Jack Trent neck deep in icy water, Jack Trent eating mealworms, Jack Trent manoeuvring his way down a treacherous rock face with accompanying waterfall. The thought of spending even one night camping alone in the middle of this freezing craggy landscape with Jack Trent made nerves flutter crazily in her stomach, and it had absolutely nothing to do with the fact that he looked like an Adonis.

'He has a cameraman tag along at various locations to film the survival-skills demonstrations, river crossings, game preparation, that kind of thing,' she said, glancing briefly across from the mud-flecked windscreen.

The words 'game preparation' rebounded sickly through Evie's mind.

'Minimal crew though—the programme isn't meant to look glossy. It's meant to look like it's thrown together. It all adds realism. Any night filming he does by himself on a handheld camera. Some of it's in diary format where he talks direct to camera. He really *is* on his own out there, not holed up in some hotel.'

There was a decidedly pointed tone to that last sentence. Was there a single member of the female species who wasn't sappily in love with Jack Trent?

'Yeah, I got that.'

If she had a quid for every time someone told her how wrong she'd got it...

'And if anything were to go wrong, which it *can't possibly*, the guy's ex-special forces. He's survived in some of the most punishing terrain in the world. He led a hostage-rescue mission in Colombia. I think he's up to managing a weekend in the Scottish Highlands with you.'

The camera was rolling even as she climbed out of the mud-splashed Jeep. Her feet in their new vice-gripping walking boots immediately sank to the ankle into the boggy ground. She followed the production assistant into a sparse brick building outside which were parked a variety of outward-bound vehicles. Crew moved around, shifting film-making equipment. So it sounded as if they took running footage and edited it down later. Fine as long as you didn't speak before thinking. She resolved to keep her wits about her.

'Have you seen any of Jack's shows before?'

'A few clips,' she said shortly. Did she look like someone who enjoyed watching people trek for miles and drink filtered urine? 'Has *he* seen any of mine?'

Clearly not. The production assistant swept on without comment.

'OK...well, first up we cover equipment, clothing, that kind of thing. Jack will work through your kit list with you. The camera will be rolling, just crack on as normal and soon you'll forget it's even there. You must be used to it anyway on your own show. We'll edit and cut as necessary, quick turnaround to make the most of the public interest. Should be able to run it in the usual *Miss Knightsbridge* prime-time slot next week.'

The camera crew assumed positions and a hand signal from the director had the filming kick in.

'*Miss Knightsbridge* is much more planned than this,' Evie said, glancing around the freezing-cold bare brickwork of the draughty room. 'It's not exactly scripted but all the locations and events are worked out beforehand. If things get a bit stilted the producer throws in a controversial topic for us all to discuss, to help things get heated. Essentially the producers stir it up.'

Her own life was really miles away from the drama it came across as on TV, not that she'd be giving that fact away. Cup-of-cocoa-quiet-life Evie was hardly likely to be of any more interest to the viewers of this show than those of her own. No way. She intended to stick to the tried and tested brash persona that had won her the prospect of an independent future before she'd stuffed it all up.

'Is that why you made that comment about me?' Jack

said, walking in. Her stomach gave a slow flip, clearly nerves at what was to come. He was fully kitted out in survival wear. Walking boots, hard-wearing trousers like her own hideous ones, jacket that looked as if it was made from a duvet. He looked as if he were about to shout a gang of squaddies through an assault course. A twist of trepidation worked its way through her stomach at what exactly the next couple of days was likely to involve. 'Because your show is a tissue of lies you assumed mine is too?'

His very first words on camera and he'd made sure they referenced her faux pas. Not even so much as a 'welcome to the show'. She watched him sorting through a pile of kit. He barely even glanced in her direction, clearly intending to be true to last night's word, doing her no favours. She shook her head a little to clear it, feeling the camera on her, annoyed with herself for trying to get him onside the previous evening. Why the hell did she need his help? Lack of encouragement wasn't exactly new to her—she'd spent half her life self-motivating to counteract her father's indifference. She'd get through this hideous experience on her own. Chester's advice flashed through her mind and she latched onto it grimly: *grovel, act contrite and come across as a game-for-anything fish out of water, sweetie. The public will lap it up.* Here was her chance to redeem herself.

'I made that comment without thinking about the consequences,' she said. She spun round to face the camera head-on. Might as well get the apology out of the way upfront. 'None of it was true,' she said clearly to the camera. 'I was stressed. It was taken out of context. I didn't make it to get at you.' She stole a look at Jack. He was watching her intently and she knew this was the part where to really regain the upper hand she should be giving a proper explanation but she simply couldn't. She wasn't about to discuss her skewed relationship with her father, not with the camera picking up every stupid nuance.

Jack kept watching her as she turned away from the camera, the blonde hair tied back, tendrils escaping and curling around her fine-boned face. His eyes strayed to the softness of her mouth before he could stop them. The full lower lip was delectable and a rush of heat sparked in his veins. He snapped his gaze away and focused hard on the kit list in front of him. He had no time for women in his life and that went double for high- maintenance ones like her. Perhaps if he put a conscious mental effort in, his body might actually get that message instead of being distracted by her.

Last night had been about playing him, about trying to charm him into making her life easier, the way she'd undoubtedly done with everyone throughout her life when things didn't go her way. He'd lost out to that kind of behaviour in the past. He certainly wouldn't be putting his trust in a TV personality with their own publicity agenda again any time soon. The way she looked was completely irrelevant.

He strengthened his resolve. After last night's attempts to manipulate him, he had the measure of her. There would be no making this easy on her, no special concessions. She was just like any other course attendee, she just happened to make a duvet jacket look sexy for once.

The camera continued to roll regardless and from the corner of his eye Jack clocked her rucksack with its gold pattern and pink straps as she hefted it onto the trestle table. She'd never make it through the weekend without walking out. There was absolutely no way.

'First rule of survival,' he said, sticking to the remit of the TV show. 'Blend in. Just how far do you think you'd get in hostile territory with that thing?' He nodded at the bag. 'You might as well have a neon flashing arrow pointing at your head.'

'It's designer,' she said, in incredulous tones, as if that gave the wearer the power of invisibility.

He strode across the sparse and draughty room, pulled a sturdy camouflage-green backpack from the stack of kit near the door and threw it to her. She caught it on reflex to stop it hitting her in the chops. It was identical to his own. He could see from the expression on her face that she loathed it on sight.

He waited expectantly until she made an irritated noise and unzipped her bulging designer rucksack. The kit list he'd provided had included no provision whatsoever for personal items. Left to him and she'd barely be allowed a toothbrush, which was really rather the point. Roughing it rather lost its mojo when you let your candidates pack luxury items.

He watched as she proceeded to remove a ludicrous selection of cosmetic items and unsuitable clothing from the rucksack, which had probably cost more than his car. Was she for real?

'Where did you think you were going?' he couldn't help saying. 'To lie by a pool in the Caribbean? You don't need a ton of designer stuff. No one does.'

'This isn't designer stuff.' She shrugged. 'Except for the rucksack. It's just everyday hygiene stuff. Lip balm, sunblock... You should be wearing Factor twenty-five, you spend so much time outdoors, or you'll look like a pensioner by the time you're fifty.' She pointed at him with the tube to press her point.

He stared at her.

'You can put it all back in your designer rucksack and hand it over to the team,' he said. 'You'll get it back when you return to base. The standard-issue kit is inside the green backpack.'

She unzipped the standard-issue backpack and peered into it.

'What the hell is this?'

He winked at her and she tried to ignore the fact that when he smiled his green eyes took on a hint of wicked melt because it made her stomach go soft. Why couldn't he have looked like some gnarly mountain man, perhaps with a beard big enough for a rodent to live in? It would make concentration on the task at hand much easier without her stomach in knots. Then again, he surely wouldn't be such a darling of the public if he looked like some hairy hillbilly.

'Torch, water bottle, purification tablets, matches, basic food rations… This is the kit I issue to all attendees of my survival course. Since you've single-handedly sabotaged my very successful business, I thought we'd use this weekend to showcase it and drum up some interest for the special kids' survival courses I'm about to launch. Essentially, you're trying out one of my courses and you owe me. So hand over the lip balm and let's get on with it.'

He held her gaze with his own, and was there a hint of enjoyment in the green eyes? Was he actually getting *off* on this? She noticed, not without a touch of admiration, that he'd managed to get in a plug for the kids' initiative thing that he was so hung up on. Maybe she should have smuggled along a bit of her jewellery and tried for a bit of product placement.

He whipped the tube of lip balm out of her hand with

a flourish, lobbed it into the designer handbag and threw the whole thing to the production minion.

Then again, she'd have been hard pressed to get as much as a necklace past him.

'And *cut*.'

She wheeled around, so absorbed in her standoff with Jack-bloody-Trent that she'd forgotten the camera was even there. Which was probably the point.

'Fantastic banter, exactly what we're looking for. Keep that up for the next couple of days and we'll be talking TV gold.'

Terrific. So all she had to do to make this stupid programme a success was to spend the entire weekend at Jack Trent's throat. Shouldn't be too difficult since he was obviously not going to cut her an inch of slack.

'Shall we?' he said, ushering her towards the door with a flourish and a wicked grin.

She trudged mutinously to the exit. The wind swept across to buffet her the second she put her nose outside the door. She followed him through the mud for a short distance until he left what passed laughably for a road and headed off across the open terrain. The camera filmed their departure as she trudged after him and then presumably the cameraman would catch up with them on the way to their first checkpoint, whatever the hell that was. Probably set up ready for the filming of some horror bush-craft task. She tried not to think about her cosy flat back in London as she hooked her gloved hands into the shoulders of her standard-issue backpack. She concentrated on walking behind Jack in the hope that his muscular bulk might cut out some of the wind.

He clearly thought he was spending the weekend with some socialite Barbie type and that she wouldn't last five minutes. She wasn't about to give him the satisfaction. She'd managed to pull off It-girl party princess with aplomb, surely she could tweak that and channel girl adventurer if she put her mind to it—exactly how hard could it be?

Biting winds, perpetual freezing drizzle. Sharp craggy rocks, inclines lined with bogs, heather, rough spiky tufts of grass, and the greyest skyline Evie had ever seen. The cameraman trudged along at a distance behind them, occasionally stopping to take shots of the skyline and surroundings that she supposed would be edited into the footage of her and Jack to give a sense of the bleak wilderness.

With the outward-bound centre long out of sight and dense trees and foliage up ahead, Jack came to a stop and offloaded his rucksack. She watched him, shifting from one foot to the other, wondering what horrible task was ahead of her. The cameraman set himself up to one side and got the film rolling.

'Like I said back at base,' Jack began, 'blending in is the first rule of survival in a hostile environment, so let's start with that. It's not just about carrying the right rucksack.'

He paused, during which the camera swept across to Evie to catch her eye-roll at the designer dig.

'There's always more ways to improvise—it's just a matter of thinking outside the box.' He looked at Evie amenably enough. 'Can you see anything in your immediate surroundings that might help?'

She pursed her lips and looked around at the craggy wilderness. She could feel the camera zooming in for a close-up of her make-up-free and undoubtedly pink-cheeked face. Annabel's advice danced through her mind. *You don't need to take this.* She squashed it hard.

'Nope,' she said.

'OK, what about this?'

He got down on one knee and scooped up a handful of mud from the nearby ditch, then in one movement drew his fingers in stripes across his face. She could imagine the nation's female contingent swooning at the sight of his mud-streaked rugged cheekbones. Just great. He looked up at her expectantly.

Oh, you must be bloody joking.

'Really?' She pulled a disbelieving face. 'You're actually suggesting *I* put that stuff on my face?'

He held up a muddy hand and failed to stop a hint of amusement lifting the corner of his mouth. So that was it. Get your own back.

'It's all about embracing the experience,' he said. 'Survival is all about stripping back all the window dressing and using what you can find around you. *Miss Knightsbridge* is all about window dressing and luxury consumer durables. Girls these days are quite happy to use fillers or have cosmetic surgery as a quick fix but you're on edge about smearing a bit of natural mud on your cheeks. Your lifestyle is obviously so far removed from what's important that all sense of initiative has gone.'

She knew perfectly well that he was simply trying to provoke a reaction from her for the camera but knowing that didn't seem to count for much when it came to keeping calm. He had absolutely no clue about her life or that the luxuries with which her father fobbed her off meant nothing because they were his way of keeping her out of his life. How the hell could she expect someone like him to understand that? He took self-sufficiency to the nth degree. He probably had no need for anyone or anything in his life to validate him. Well, lucky, *lucky* him.

Before she knew what she was doing his self-righteous judgemental claptrap tipped her temper into the red and she was on her knees at his feet, water soaking through the awful trousers at both knees. She leaned into the ditch and scooped up a massive blob of the mud in each hand, then stood up and looked him right in the eye as she held her hands up. He took a defensive step backwards at the implication that she was about to lob it in a huge splat at his grinning face and if it hadn't been for the knowledge that Jack Trent's fan base would probably issue a lynch mob, she might have done exactly that.

Instead she drew herself up to her full height and worked survival girl for all she was worth.

'For your information,' she shouted, 'I do *not*...' pause to slap a huge wodge of the cold oozy mud on her left cheek '...use fillers!' She slapped another handful on her right cheek and swirled the hideous stuff over her chin and forehead. It felt cold and gritty against her skin, its damp and earthy smell filling her nostrils.

The cameraman, clearly desperate to record every nuance of her mud-smothered expression, was in her personal space and she shoved him hard enough in the chest that he sat down with a squelch and the lens zipped sharply upwards to take in a random shot of the grey cloud-filled sky. The soundtrack wasn't affected and Evie's exasperated yell was clearly audible.

'Get that thing out of my face!'

Jack watched as she lifted her backpack and channelled defiance so palpable he could feel it. Her eyes looked bluer than ever in her muddy face. A spike of heat fired up low in his stomach. In that animated moment when she'd smeared the mud, flashing anger lighting up her eyes and the wind whipping her golden hair every which way, she'd looked absolutely magnificent.

He'd based his impression of Evie entirely on her rich background and expensive lifestyle. How could a girl with an unattainable life, who'd been handed everything on a plate, possibly be a good role model? Helen's phone call crossed his mind. *Evie Staverton-Lynch is really cool and funny.* On some level the ludicrous Knightsbridge show had engaged the viewing public, girls like Helen. And against his expectation, Evie hadn't walked off set at the first sign of hard work. A tiny spark of cautious admiration flared. She had some defiance and drive about her. Was that so bad an example to girls like Helen? His judgement of her went back to the drawing board.

Ten minutes later and the cameraman walked behind them at a safe distance, lens cap firmly on. The wind had dropped a little, just a *little,* mind you, and the drying mud felt gritty on her cheeks.

Glancing sideways she saw that Jack was grinning at her, that lopsided delicious grin that melted the hearts of the nation's women. She raised eyebrows at him.

'What?'

'Nothing. I just wasn't convinced you'd run with the camouflage thing.' His voice sounded a hell of a lot warmer than it had throughout this whole hideous experience so far. 'You know, after last night's request to go easy on you.'

Had to keep bringing that up, didn't he?

'No kidding.' Her cheeks felt facepack-tight with the gritty drying mud. 'Was I supposed to walk off the show at the first hurdle? Sorry to disappoint.'

A small boost of triumph spurred her on. She wasn't

going to give *anyone* the satisfaction of being able to say she was a lightweight. It was mind over matter, that was all.

'You didn't disappoint,' he said, then shrugged. 'That was actually pretty cool.'

She didn't reply, surprised at the prick of satisfaction that comment caused, because really she didn't care one bit what Jack Trent thought about her.

'And I never thought you did,' he said.

She frowned.

'Did what?'

He looked sideways at her, the grin touching his eyes now too. Even smothered in mud he was drop-dead gorgeous—how absolutely *unfair.*

'Use Botox. I was just talking it up for the camera, trying to psych you up. Sometimes on the courses you have to get in there and motivate people or they just give up before they've begun.'

It irked her that he'd just assumed she would have walked away rather than smear a bit of mud on her face if he hadn't talked her up. For some reason it had bothered her from the beginning that he bought so easily into the spoilt-brat image she'd built up in the media, instantly dismissing that there could possibly be anything more to her than shallow It-girl *Miss Knightsbridge.*

In the last year, with the show at the pinnacle of its success, she'd become used to people being delighted to meet her and had assembled a wide circle of ego-boosting friends who told her whatever she wanted to hear. The diva-socialite persona that had done so well at charming the public seemed to do absolutely zilch to impress Jack Trent. He simply accepted the stereotype at face value. He'd assumed she'd never be up to tackling this weekend under her own steam. But how could she blame him for taking her at face value when that was the face she'd chosen to put on?

And why the hell did she even care? It wasn't as if their paths would ever cross again after this weekend. Unless the stupid show won an award.

'Let's get one thing straight,' she snapped. 'I don't need psyching up, thanks very much. I certainly didn't slap mud on my face because of anything *you* said. I was just…sizing up the situation before I got stuck in. I'm perfectly capable of getting through whatever you throw at me.'

He held both hands up.

'OK, OK. I'm sure you are. I didn't mean to imply otherwise. I just wasn't sure how you'd take to this stuff, what with you being so…' she waited as he floundered, poised to sink his foot back into his mouth, eventually choosing '…city based.' She pushed a hand through her hair. Hmm. Could have been worse.

Another few minutes of silent trudging and her stomach twisted into a knot of tension. He'd tried to be friendly and she'd knocked him back. She felt a pang of regret now. However hideous the tasks were likely to be, she was on her own with him for the bulk of the next two days. That would be a whole lot easier if they were at least on friendly terms.

'You didn't answer my question,' she said.

He looked sideways at her.

'Question?'

'Last night. How *does* someone get into this kind of thing?' she asked. 'I mean, look at this place. It's freezing, cold, wet.' She waved a hand at her own face. 'We're covered in mud, for Pete's sake. People actually *pay* you to come and do this stuff?'

She shifted her backpack a little to make it a fraction less uncomfortable.

He gave her an amused sideways glance at her sudden interest after the grouching of a few minutes earlier and she shrugged and gave him a half-smile.

'We're stuck with each other for the next forty-eight hours. We may as well make some kind of attempt to get along.'

'A real attempt, you mean? Or a manipulative style attempt to get me to go easy on you?'

'A real attempt,' she said. 'But you can't blame me for trying.'

'I don't blame you.' He caught her eye and gave her a wicked smile that crinkled the edges of his green eyes. Her stomach give an unexpected flip in response and she gripped the straps of her rucksack hard. 'If you feel like trying again, don't let me stop you.'

Her stomach was in full flip-flop mode now.

'Not that it will get you any special treatment. I've dealt with people like you in the past. I'm immune to any charm offensive.'

'People like me?'

Her flipping stomach lurched to a halt. Just what the hell did *that* mean?

'TV stars. Darlings of the media. So seduced by the idea of fame that the real world passes them by.'

Angry warmth crept upward from the turned-up collar of her coat at the injustice of that and the accompanying frustration that *she* was the one who'd cultivated that very impression. He was simply taking her TV image at face value, assuming there was nothing more to her than clothes-obsessed party girl. She turned to him indignantly, unable to focus on the fact that she really shouldn't care what the hell he thought of her.

'You don't know the first thing about me,' she said.

'I know everything I need to know. Just the fact you're doing this show speaks volumes.' He shrugged. 'I'm not making a judgement. Each to their own.'

His short cryptic answers made him impossible to read, just like her father. Did they offer training on that in the military? Was there some kind of bloody *course*?

'I'm doing it, among other reasons, to save *your* arse,' she pointed out irritably.

His amenable attitude melted away like smoke and she held up her hands as he stared at her.

'No, no. No need to thank me,' she said.

'Thank you? You're the one who caused all this trouble in the first place with your bloody à la carte comment.'

'Which I've apologised for so many times now that I've lost count. Has it occurred to you that I could just have refused to go ahead with this charade of a TV show, just left your reputation in tatters instead of trying to put things right?'

'Of course it's occurred to me. It's not like you need the money, is it? But you're obviously so wrapped up in your own fame that you couldn't possibly contemplate leaving the *Evil Evie* image intact, so you've agreed to do this in the hope it will redress the balance. And heaven forbid that there might actually be anything deeper to it all than what the best choice is for your TV success.'

He kept walking at the same grim trudging pace, eyes now fixed straight ahead of him. She had to work to keep up with his stride.

'I'm no different from you,' she panted. 'You said it yourself—you've only kept your TV shows up because the publicity feeds into your own business, these damn survival courses of yours. You need your public image just as much as I do to keep your profits up, so don't try and take the moral high ground. I have my own reasons for doing the TV show and they have nothing to do with being fame crazed.'

He came to a sudden standstill and she nearly crashed into him with the momentum she'd built up in keeping pace.

'You think what I do is about making a *profit*?' he snapped. 'Why am I even surprised?' He shook his head disbelievingly and looked skyward. 'I've spent years organising charity expeditions, rounding up donations from people like you who are only interested in what's in it for them. And this new kids' initiative will be non-profit-making for me. Everything that comes from it will be ploughed right back in. Because actually there's more important things in life than counting your bank balance.' He paused and then added in contempt, 'Or your social media followers.'

He strode off again and this time she didn't try and keep up.

CHAPTER FOUR

FOUR HOURS IN and it was freeze-your-arse-off cold, and not just from the elements. The vibes coming from Jack Trent were icy and why was she even surprised? Ex-military, just like her father. Uncommunicative, giving nothing away. No discussion, no opportunity to hear her reasons for being here. Just his own assumptions about her and her situation. And his opinion was apparently the only one with any validity.

The churn of unease in her stomach refused to let up. Channelling self-righteous should come easily to the made-for-TV version of herself. *Miss Knightsbridge*'s It-girl Evie wouldn't give a toss about offending Jack Trent. She certainly wouldn't apologise for it. But it seemed to be getting harder to hang onto that carefully crafted persona out here, away from all the luxury trappings of her London life, without yes-people hanging around her for handy validation. Was she really bothered about upsetting him, about his good opinion of her? Or did it have more to do with how she felt about herself right now? Everyone wanted to be liked, Evie included, and with him shooting daggers her way she felt a little as if she were back at her first day at school.

He let his pace flounder for a brief instant while he

unfastened his water bottle and she took advantage of the situation to catch him up.

'I'm sorry,' she said quickly, before he could stride off again. 'For what I said before. I didn't realise your kids' course was non-profit. And all your charity stuff... I read about that on the Internet. I didn't mean to disrespect all that.'

There. Job done. She felt better for it. The public might still want to hang her out to dry but at least in her own mind she wouldn't be Evil Evie, undermining charitable benefits for the nation's kids. He was staring at her in surprise and she shifted her backpack a little, uncomfortable under his gaze.

He recapped the water bottle and swiped the back of his hand across his lips, one eye on her, sizing her up. An apology? He hadn't seen that coming.

He inclined his head a little in acknowledgement and she offered him a cautious smile.

'Look, I know neither of us would be in this situation if it weren't for me,' she said. 'I made this mess and I'll sort it out. I'm not about to walk off set. I'll finish the show, make it clear what I said wasn't true, and hopefully your kids' courses won't be affected.' She unfastened her backpack and fished her own water bottle from inside it. 'Just don't expect me to exclaim in delight for the camera when I have to roll in the mud or eat bugs. I'll do the tasks and at the end we'll be all square—right?'

She kept her eyes on him as she took a sip of the drink, clearly gauging his reaction. Jack was surprised. She'd held her hands up instead of letting it slide. He'd regretted his outburst as soon as it happened, regretted losing it when he'd never expected her to give a flying toss about his charity work anyway.

'I may have overreacted,' he conceded carefully.

She frowned at him questioningly as she recapped her water bottle.

'How so?'

He leaned down to his backpack and shifted the contents around a little for a better fit.

'I don't exactly have a fantastic track record with people in the public eye.'

The frown stayed in place as she waited for him to elaborate.

'I ran a charity expedition a couple of years ago,' he said, glancing up at her. 'A trek to the summit of Mount Kilimanjaro. I managed to garner quite a bit of interest, had a few army mates going, a couple of ex sports stars.' He paused. 'And a TV presenter. Great for raising public awareness if you can persuade a few people in the public eye to do it, really increases the money raised.'

He didn't name names although his irritation had never gone away.

'Anyway, an outing like that takes a lot of organisation. Safety planning, travel costs. I was quite en vogue at the time. The *Extreme* TV shows had just taken off.' He gave a wry smile at the thought. The whole TV personality thing had come as quite a shock at the time. He hadn't reckoned on the hungry public interest in outdoor pursuits at a time when online gaming and technology had opened up access for kids to a whole new world without even leaving the house. 'The TV presenter who was coming along had just written his autobiography. He obviously saw it as a way of getting a bit more exposure. I was fine with that. His coming along would raise awareness of the cause—publicity works both ways, right?'

She nodded.

'Anyway, everything was in place, we were just getting ready to announce our line-up, hoping the sponsorships would roll in, and the TV guy drops out.'

He stood up and hefted his backpack into place.

'At the last minute?' She shoved her water bottle back in her own bag and hauled it onto her shoulders.

He nodded and began walking. He took it easier, letting her stay alongside him.

'If it had been an injury or something, it wouldn't have been an issue. Last thing I would have done is taken someone along who wasn't physically fit. He'd apparently decided that the nature of the charitable cause wasn't a good enough fit.'

'You're kidding?' There was incredulous laughter in her voice.

He nodded his head.

'I know. I couldn't believe it. Young people's drug rehabilitation was "too gritty".' He held up his hands and made sarcastic speech marks in the air. 'Next thing I know, he's taking part in some cycle ride for a children's hospital. I know that's a perfectly great cause, and good luck to them. What I'm saying is, for this person, it had nothing to do with supporting a charity. He wanted the publicity for his own end. And at the last minute support for teenagers with drug problems wasn't sympathetic enough for him so he looked for another cause that was a bit more fluffy bunny.'

'That's absolutely outrageous,' she said. 'What happened to the expedition?'

He shrugged.

'It went ahead. But we definitely lost out on publicity. Ergo we lost out on donations. I wasn't happy.'

His rabid drive when it came to his charity work had never been stronger than, ironically, when there was someone else letting the side down.

'I can imagine.'

'It was basically all about him. All about his image.' He looked at her, walking alongside him with her hands hooked into her backpack straps. 'You started out here acting the diva after your comments had caused all this trouble for my kids' initiative and then you go and imply I'm just in it all for the profits. I saw red.' He paused. 'I appreciate the apologies. All of them. And that you're prepared to do all you can to redress the situation.'

He looked sideways at her, at the heart-shaped face with its smears of mud as she kept up the pace. She smiled at him as she nodded her acknowledgement and his stomach softened. She looked much younger and more fragile without make-up and with the huge back-pack weighing her down. She seemed determined to try and put things right, to rectify the damage she'd caused. He of all people could respect that and respond to it. He smiled back.

Evie concentrated on putting one foot in front of the other. No wonder Jack hadn't exactly been Mr Support-ive so far—he'd probably been waiting for her to jump ship like that awful TV person he'd mentioned. Her dis-gust at the story he'd told her mingled with uneasiness that he'd so easily been able to form that exact same conclusion about her. In it for herself, with no thought or regard for anyone else. Despite the success of her TV show and the independence it had brought her, did she really want to be *that* person?

She could see the minimal film crew up ahead way before she reached them and her stomach began to lurch hideously. There was obviously some kind of task just ready and waiting for her to make a fool of herself on camera. She arranged her face carefully into a neutral couldn't-give-a-toss-what-you-throw-at-me expression.

As she neared the group she could see the ground beyond falling away, and then the tangled pile of harnesses at the foot of the launch area. A zip wire had been constructed, clearly to transport them down to the lower level where the terrain looked even more craggy and damp than it did up here. If that was possible. Worst of all, the zip was massively long and at least fifty feet off the ground. It felt suddenly as if her bladder were gripped in a vice, and she turned away, trying to get her nerves under control, trying not to hyperventilate and give herself away.

'Everything all right?' Jack put a hand on her arm and as she glanced down at it he squeezed gently. Genuine concern. His voice was perfectly calm. 'This is absolutely safe. Tried and tested. Nothing to worry about, you just step off the edge and enjoy the ride.' He smiled at her encouragingly and she attempted a smile in return that came out as more of a grimace.

'*Enjoy* it?' Was he mad?

'We can take as long as you need.'

He searched her face, his expression serious, and the nervous churning in her stomach subsided slightly. Of course, he was the consummate professional. This care and concern was nothing special, certainly not just for her; he was probably like it with everyone. People needed to be able to look at that face and trust that when they stepped off that edge on his watch, they wouldn't plummet fifty feet to the ground.

'And you don't have to do this,' he added. 'It's not set in stone.'

Did she imagine the edge in his voice there? No, it wasn't set in stone but they both knew what was at stake here. Yes, she could still back out; no one was making her do this. She thought of that selfish TV presenter who screwed Jack Trent over for his own benefit. She could be that person. All she'd need to do was call this whole thing off.

She could disappear from the show and take the sacking from Purple Productions. Let the lease on her jewellery shop go and return to living off her allowance. Her father would be happy. She would be under control. He probably wouldn't need to contact her for a couple of years if she behaved well enough. With a fifty-foot drop just feet away that thought lost some of its usual sting. Walking away would be so easy.

From somewhere deep inside enough pride bubbled up to counteract the temptation.

'I'm good,' she managed. 'What do I have to do?'

For all the bravado and the breezy smile she flashed at the camera, he could tell she was nervous. It was in her eyes when she approached the edge of the drop to put the harness on.

'OK?' he said, kneeling down. She leaned on him for balance and he was suddenly very aware of her hand as it crept around his neck in a shaky grip and those long, long legs as he helped her step into the harness. When he stood up to slip the straps high up on her thighs they seemed to go on for ever. Another strap circled her waist and his mind insisted on registering how slender she was beneath the loose outdoor clothing as he held her steady and tightened the fastening. His mouth felt oddly dry.

'I'm fine.' Her voice was pinched and brittle. Not fine.

He glanced up from the harness to see her looking up at him, her face just inches from his own, the high cheekbones pale, and she offered him a smile that smacked of fright. His heart skipped a little at that. He liked her for not being that person who backed out.

'Just lean back into it and let yourself go,' he said, reaching up to clip her harness to the metal pulley on the wire.

Channelling outdoor girl as if her life depended on it, Evie pressed her lips together and vice-gripped the line attaching her harness to the zip wire. She locked her eyes with Jack's green ones and tried to focus on how calm he was. His career was obviously everything to him; he wasn't about to let her die on his watch. She leaned back, as instructed, and as her boots left solid ground she couldn't hold in a scream.

'Oh, bloody *heeeeeeellllll...*'

Her voice was swept away by the wind the instant it left her lips.

Back on the ledge, the director let out an exasperated noise.

'Oh, that's just great. We'll have to bleep that out. Did no one tell her about swearing before the watershed?'

At the end of the landing site one of Jack's outward-bound crew unfastened Evie from the wire and she immediately sank to the ankle into the boggy ground. Even feet soaked in mud couldn't detract from the utter, unexpected triumph she felt at having got through the task without looking too much of a sap. She punched the air in victory. She could do this. She was *owning* this experience.

Two minutes later and she watched Jack speed down the wire, posture perfect, not a flailing limb or a yell in sight, unclipping himself expertly the moment he hit the end. He handed his harness to the crew and headed towards her. She couldn't stop a smile bubbling onto her lips.

'I'm impressed,' he said, grinning back. 'I could tell you were nervous but I knew you could do it.'

That gorgeous lopsided grin and those crinkling eyes instantly made her stomach flip and she pressed her hands against her middle. That she was liking him more had *nothing* to do with finding him attractive. It was just the novelty of having someone believe in her and encourage her for once. The *real* her too, in a situation that stripped bare any made-for-TV bravado. Not the invented designer version of her in an invented designer situation.

'I was *not* nervous,' she said, then realised how mad that sounded. She'd screamed the entire distance of the zip. She shrugged. 'Maybe I was, a little. I never did anything like that before. Even the times I went camping as a kid, something like that would have been way out of my league.' She pulled her water bottle from her backpack and took a sip. 'Maybe you're onto something with those kids' courses of yours. My brother would have been mad for that zip wire experience when we were kids.'

She thought briefly of Will, away on tour in the Middle East. Not that he needed to be thrill seeking now. He had enough danger in his working life.

'You went camping as a kid? *You?*'

Jack was looking at her in surprise and she held out a hand, mildly exasperated.

'No need to look so amazed. You'd never know it to look at me now but I could climb a tree with the best of them,' she said. 'I was a real tomboy.'

'Some rich campsite on the sunny continent?' he asked.

'No. Come rain or shine, in Devon or Cornwall,' she countered, noticing the raise of his eyebrows. 'My mother liked traditional seaside holidays at home. Rock pools, ice cream, camping. Just like the ones she'd had as a kid. She was quite big on building family traditions.'

An unexpected prickle of dull longing made her press her lips together hard. She didn't revisit the past very much in her mind, certainly not out loud. Looking back didn't change anything; there was no point pining now for what might have been. No choice but to make the best of what was left.

'Sounds great,' he said, zipping up his backpack.

'It was.'

A tug of nostalgia made her mouth feel dry and she swallowed hard. How long had it been since she'd thought of those times? Climbing trees, pestering Will to let her go fishing with him. The fun and closeness of her early childhood had degenerated until her part in the family was now little more than a public façade. There was no sense of belonging, no matter how hard she looked for it.

'I assumed you would have a holiday home in Barbados or something.' His tone was matter-of-fact. It seemed that for him she really *was* that stereotype. Rich holidays, luxury lifestyle. He thought he knew her already because her TV image preceded her. She found she didn't like that one bit. 'Sounds like you spent more time in the great outdoors as a kid than I did,' he said.

'I imagined *you* to be outside in all weathers virtually from babyhood,' she said. 'Practically born in a tent. Or maybe a shelter built from sticks. Aren't your family all mad for the outdoor life too?'

He replaced his jacket and hauled his backpack into place, not looking at her. She did the same, ready to get moving, spurred on now by the adrenaline of doing the zip-wire plunge, by the reassuring thought that *she could do this*.

He shook his head as they left the zip wire behind them, equipment being packed up now by the production team.

'We didn't really do family holidays,' Jack said shortly. They hadn't done an awful lot of family anything.

Onward now just the two of them for a while, a cameraman lagging behind. He was tensely aware of her, walking next to him with a new burst of confidence after going through with the zip wire. It was one of the highlights of his work, watching people overcome their fears and push themselves, watching them be pleased with the results. Encouraging people to see their potential. Redress on some small level, he hoped, for caring only about his own potential in the past.

'The outdoor stuff came about more from my army years,' he said, steering the conversation neatly around his childhood. Not his finest years. 'I was in the forces for a long time.'

She nodded.

'I knew you were in the army,' she said. 'I read it online. There's stuff on there about your survival courses, a little bit about your background.' She paused. 'If you pick your way between the photos of you with starlets and models on your arm, that is.'

He glanced her way in time to see her wink at him. It never failed to amaze him the ludicrous media interest that was shown in who he happened to be dating. If only the same publicity could be given to his fund-raising. His mind lit on the fact that she'd done some research on him, surprised that she would take the time. His overall assumption about her had been that she was too absorbed by her own life to think about anyone or anything else.

'The army is...' He searched for the right words to describe that section of his life, long behind him now. It had been an escape route at first. And later much more than that. 'A way of life,' he said eventually. 'I worked abroad a lot, in some very isolated places for long periods of time. You're cut off from reality in situations like that.'

'Reality?'

'Family,' he said briefly. 'The day-to-day stuff.'

He really had no desire to discuss his background with anyone, let alone with someone who could hardly relate to a need to escape from anything. She was born into a rich family and she'd had the best of everything delivered to her on a plate. He doubted she'd ever had to fight for anything or anyone.

'That sounds familiar,' she said. He looked at her in surprise and she shrugged. 'My father is ex-army too. My brother's still serving. Uncles and grandfather. Military is a big watchword in my family.'

There was a bitter edge to her voice that he couldn't fail to miss and that piqued his curiosity.

'Then you'll know it's more than a job. It's a life, really. That's why I joined up.' He thought back down the years to that decision. A way out, that was what his grandfather had called it. He hadn't realised at the time it would end up being at the expense of so much. 'I hadn't had much direction in my teens, didn't do well at school. I was...drifting really.'

Drifting? He had to stifle a mad laugh. He had no idea where that word had come from. Drifting was what you did when you backpacked around Asia, not what you did when you started with boredom and bad company and slid into petty crime, with a long-term potential for not-so-petty crime. Not that he had any inclination to enlighten her or anyone else about his past mess.

'The army changed everything,' he said. 'For six years I lived this completely different life. The friendship, the team ethic, the physical demands of it were exactly what I needed. Exactly what I wanted.'

'If it was so fantastic, why on earth did you leave?' she said.

He saw that one coming. She wasn't the first person to ask. He cleared his throat.

'Like I said, it isolates you from your home life.' *If you let it.* 'I had responsibilities to get back to. But from the moment I left I missed the challenge, the teamwork, that kind of stuff.'

'Is that why you do those charity expeditions? I was surprised at how much charity stuff you do.'

He paused to look at her, eyebrows raised.

'You're a celebrity,' she said and he saw her notice his wince. 'Like it or not. You have a Wikipedia page. It wasn't hard. I just did a web search on you.'

'Why? To see what you were in for?'

She shook her head.

'To see what you were really like. When you haven't got off on the wrong foot because someone's insulted you.'

'And?'

When he glanced her way she smiled and tilted her head to one side as if she was sizing him up. The gesture was very cute. Beneath the streaks of dried mud her cheeks and the tip of her nose were pink with the cold and the blue eyes were bright and smart. To look at that delectable soft lower lip was to wonder how it might feel and taste to kiss her. Heat curled through his body at that maddeningly recurring thought.

'It didn't really help, to be honest,' Evie said.

When it came to Jack Trent the Internet was big on smoking-hot pictures of him but disappointingly short on juicy detail. 'There's lots of stuff about your TV shows and charity expeditions, a ton of photos of you with various girls on your arm, and hardly anything about the man behind all that. Then there's the outdoorsy websites banging on about how harrowing your survival courses are. I stopped reading after that.'

He grinned a little at that. It made the corners of his eyes crease and lit his face. He really was so gorgeous.

'Maybe that's the only stuff worth knowing,' he said. 'The expeditions have been great. The thing about leaving the army was that suddenly that team ethic had gone. I missed the challenge, missed pushing myself. And a sense of purpose. The charity things were a way of doing some good. Then the survival courses followed on from that.' He shrugged. 'We all need to make a living. Those of us without trust funds anyway.'

'Ha-bloody-ha,' she said. 'The need to make a living doesn't have to just be about money.'

'Only someone who doesn't need money could possibly say that,' he said.

She smiled a little.

'There's only so much shopping and schmoozing you can do before it becomes a bit directionless,' she said.

He leaned in close to her and lowered his voice. Her stomach gave a flutter at the sudden unexpected closeness.

'Watch there isn't a camera switched on,' he said.

'That kind of talk really doesn't fit your socialite-princess image.'

Heat rose in her cheeks at the astute expression on his face.

CHAPTER FIVE

SAME SKELETON FILM crew, different location. Same churning of nerves in Evie's stomach. This time there was some shelter from the trees and rocks. Jack delivered an introduction to the camera and it panned away from him to take in the murky green water of the river that flowed behind them, trees and foliage lining its muddy banks. On a sunny day in the height of summer she supposed it might have looked inviting. Right now it just looked hideously cold. She loitered to one side under the dripping pine trees.

'There are rules to follow when it comes to river crossings,' he said to the camera. 'It's extremely important to find the best location to cross safely. Make sure you've assessed your exit route on the opposite bank, allowing extra space for some drift in case you're pulled downstream once you're in the water.'

Her mind stuttered to a standstill as it processed those last words and she walked into shot before she realised what she was doing.

'Did you just say "in the water"?' she said. 'As in you and me? No bridge? No stepping stones?'

He smiled and nodded at her interaction, always the perfect professional.

'There are a number of ways you can approach it, but,

yes, one of them is to wade across. That's what we'll be demonstrating today. So the location you choose is key. You need to be aware of river debris and current. And you need to keep as much of your kit dry as you possibly can.'

He stepped away from her, the camera following his every move, and unzipped his outer jacket, all the while holding her gaze with his own. Whether that was meant to be seen as challenging or encouraging she had no idea, she was far too busy watching as he followed the jacket up by reaching behind his head and tugging off his thin fleece pullover. Droplets of moisture clung to his hair. Beneath the pullover was a sludge-green T-shirt that clung to every contour of his heavily muscled chest and torso and picked out the green of his eyes to boot. Her jaw felt suddenly as if it were loose and she was sure she wasn't alone. She could just imagine the nation's women putting off making that cup of tea just for a few minutes to see *exactly* how many garments Jack Trent might remove.

He continued talking to camera as he stripped, banging on about crossing the river at a forty-five-degree angle as if anyone *cared* when he was removing his underlying T-shirt to reveal the tightest, most toned abs and chest she'd ever seen. Her tongue crept into the corner of her mouth and she realised both he and the camera were looking at her expectantly. Oh, crap. Had he asked her a question? What had she missed?

'Ultimately the aim is to keep your clothes as dry as possible, so you undress to the minimum layer you can manage,' he repeated.

He looked at her expectantly.

She held up a finger.

'Could we just...' she beckoned him over to her

'...one moment. Quick discussion?' The cameraman followed and she scowled at him.

Jack's skin was taut and tanned and she swallowed hard as she leaned in to speak to him privately.

'What's up?' he said. 'Make it quick. It's bloody freezing.' He shifted from foot to foot in his shorts, his breath coming in fast audible bursts.

She shook her head at him.

'Are you actually expecting *me* to undress?' she said. 'On camera? I thought I'd better check.'

'It's a serious documentary,' he said, as if stripping to your underwear on prime-time TV was perfectly acceptable. 'It's practical. It's not about titillation.'

'You're joking,' she said. 'Half the women in the country will be freeze-framing you.'

He gave an exasperated eye-roll.

'There's no need to get naked,' he said. 'Just the outer layers. This is standard for every single course I run. It's an absolutely fundamental survival skill.' He paused. 'But if you're really not up for it, that's fine too. I'll do the crossing solo.'

His smile was reassuring. He looked as if he were in his element and suddenly all she wanted was to go home to her cosy flat, take a long hot bath and curl up in her pyjamas. And possibly never go out again. As if falling out of nightclubs had ever been her pastime of choice. The whole *Miss Knightsbridge* social-bunny image was a means to an end, no more. Her stepping stone to independence. The producers wouldn't have looked twice at her if they'd known her real clothing of choice was loungewear. She gritted her teeth.

'The public would love that, wouldn't they? I do the show from the sidelines instead of getting involved.'

'Sod the viewing public. Your remit is to guest on the

show—doesn't mean you have to take part in every bit of it. I never expect anyone to undertake a task unless they're absolutely sure about it.'

The location director hastily joined them.

'But the more you take part in, the better it will look,' she pointed out.

'There are safety issues to think about,' Jack countered. 'River crossings are tough. The segment will still work if I go it alone.'

His support brought a surge of warmth. There she was thinking he might enjoy seeing her submerged in horrible river water and when it came down to it he was the only one here in her corner. There was no compromising on safety, not on his watch. He was looking out for her. That more than anything made her go ahead. She wanted to show him she was up to the challenge.

'Are you sure you don't want to give this one a miss?'

'And let you have all the fun in that freezing river?' She laughed manically.

The TV crew exchanged resigned glances and it was clear they were expecting, no, scratch that, *hoping* for some kind of diva tantrum. It was obvious she hadn't been properly briefed about what the show would involve, undoubtedly so the camera could record the full shock value when each task was revealed. She'd started out a bit shakily with the 'mud on the face' thing, but since then he found himself admiring her more and more for throwing herself into it.

Now she was unzipping her thick outer jacket in his peripheral vision and he found it nigh on impossible to make his eyes look anywhere but at her. He forced himself to concentrate on rolling up his own discarded clothes and piling them into the waterproof backpack.

When his eyes traitorously strayed back towards her, she was tugging her own fleece top over her head, followed up by a T-shirt. Underneath was a black vest top and clinging shorts that made her perfectly toned legs look longer than ever. He could imagine her jogging around Hyde Park in the sunshine in designer sportswear, top-of-the-range MP3 player plugged into her ears, and he latched onto that image hard. They were from totally different worlds and he needed to keep his head. That would be so much easier if she weren't exactly what he went for in terms of looks: fit and sporty and especially now without the extra gloss of the make-up and hairstyling.

'OK?' He managed to peel his tongue from the roof of his mouth and speak.

'Let's just get it over with,' she said, through chattering teeth. 'It's freezing and we're not even in the sodding water yet.'

He distracted himself by talking up the task requirements as he climbed down the river bank.

'You need a location with good footholds on both sides of the river with a broad exit area,' he said. 'Backpack over one shoulder only, facing downstream, so you can dump it if you need to in case you lose your footing.'

He held a hand up to her and after a moment she took it and climbed down next to him, her feet sinking into the gritty mud.

'Just follow my lead,' he said loudly, over the soft rush of the water. 'Take it steady.'

It was too cold to speak. The icy water seemed to squeeze all the breath out of her as Evie pressed her teeth together and plunged into the water behind him. She shrieked as the water slopped above waist height. There was a light current tugging at her legs, wanting to pull her downstream, and she concentrated hard on leaning against it, following Jack's path. Mud oozed grittily between her numb toes and clouded up around her through the water. Every step involved a teetering balancing act with her backpack and her bodyweight versus the pull of the undertow.

The cold was unbelievable but still she thought she was holding her own. In only a few minutes Jack's backpack was thrown onto the opposite bank, and he'd pulled himself out of the water. The camera recorded every detail.

'Think about finding a good strong foothold,' he called back to her.

She grabbed at a tuft of grass with one hand and put her weight on her left foot, all ready to pull herself out, early triumph kicking in that she'd *done* this. She even had a fleeting moment to be grateful that he'd gone first so he wouldn't be behind her and watching her backside as she flailed about and tried to get out, and then the current ruined it all by sweeping the mud out from under her foot and she fell back into the river with a reeling splash.

She surfaced with a spluttering scream and floundered to find her footing. Her backpack floated away on its own. And, OK, so it wasn't exactly white water and they'd obviously dumbed down their river choice to novice level, but with its icy-cold temperature and shifting muddy bed it was hard to pull herself back to a standing position. Dark panic rose in her chest as she tried to grab for the bank, for anything at all, all the while feeling colder and drifting further downstream, and then he was suddenly there. A huge splash as he threw himself straight back into the water and plunged towards her, arms pumping at his sides to propel himself along until he reached her. Pulling her into a standing position until she was on her feet, he shouted instructions into her ear and moved behind her to push her towards the bank, where the production team had dropped everything to help. Unfortunately with the exception of the cameraman, eagerly recording every dripping-wet and humiliating moment.

As they landed on the bank, Jack right next to her, both of them soaking wet and smeared with mud, there was a spattering of claps from the small production team. And then she realised his arm was curled tightly around her waist and she was holding his hand in a vice grip in her own numb fingers.

'Get me a towel!' he snapped at a production assistant. Then he was wrapping it around her shoulders and rubbing her goosebumpy arms vigorously. Someone else swept in with a flask of coffee. His concern for her, putting her safety above everything else, brought a surge of happiness that warmed her to her icy cold toes. Just the basic sensation of having someone concerned about her, let alone someone who would haul arse through a freezing river to help her, was a totally alien feeling.

'If I'd known there'd be coffee I might have lost my bloody footing at the beginning,' she managed.

He sat next to her on the soft mud of the river bank while the crew packed up their kit. Tendrils of her hair still clung damply to her neck but he was glad to see that her lips had lost their blue tinge and her cheekbones had a bit more colour. He'd stood over the cameraman while she changed back into dry clothes behind one of the trees, every so often catching a glimpse of her with two corners of the towel clamped between her chin and her chest to preserve her modesty. No entourage tending to her every whim, no stylist. And no complaints.

Still she hadn't asked once if she could jack in the

show. There was no grumbling, she simply nodded whenever he asked if she was OK. Her sense of humour hadn't disappeared. His opinion of her quietly rose.

'You did really well,' he said. It didn't raise a smile and he leaned in towards her and gently bumped her shoulder with his to make her look at him. 'You did,' he repeated.

She looked sideways at him and pulled her thick jacket more tightly around her.

'I made a colossal moose of myself,' she countered. 'It wasn't exactly the Zambezi in spate, was it? Yes, there was a bit of a current but a twelve-year-old kid could probably have crossed that river without a hitch.'

'You'd be surprised,' he said. 'The cold makes everything much harder. Your heart rate spins up, you're so busy coping with how freezing you suddenly are that thinking about where to put your feet isn't the piece of cake it seems when you're watching from the bank.'

'But I wanted to get through every task with full marks,' she said, not looking at him. Instead she fixed her eyes on the river as it flowed past. 'Show people there's more to me than the shopping-obsessed diva who bad-mouthed the national treasure.'

He laughed awkwardly, never comfortable with the public approval.

'National treasure? That's a new one. Flavour of the month, more like. That's why I've tried to use the TV show to boost the charity work as much as I can—you never know when the public will get fed up with you.'

'I didn't help, did I?' she said. 'With my stupid comments. I'm really sorry.'

Her voice was defeated, no sign of the in-your-face diva now. The apology made his heart turn over in his chest.

'It's probably done good,' he said. 'Like that insane PR guy said, the one that follows you around: there's no such thing as bad publicity. If you want to feel appreciated maybe you're looking in the wrong place—the public are too fickle for words. You should be interested in what your family think, the people that care about you. I bet they'd be as proud as hell that you haven't walked away from those comments and you've gone through with this show.'

She pulled a sceptical face.

'Maybe.'

It was clear from her tone that she'd only agreed with him to fob him off. He wondered again exactly where her family was in all of this. Were they all too worried about distancing themselves from the scandal to offer her a bit of support?

'Come on,' he said, standing up. He held his hands out, keeping them there until she took them, and then he tugged her to her feet next to him.

She looked steadily into his face.

'What now?'

'We put the river behind us and get on with the next task. Just one more segment to film before we camp for the night and you give it your best shot, like you have done with all these tasks so far. You can do this. OK, so you're pissed off that you lost your footing on the river crossing but let's not lose sight of the fact you actually *got into the water.* You're doing great.'

He got a small smile this time.

'OK.'

'Great.' He put an arm around her shoulders and gave a squeeze of encouragement. Big mistake. She leaned in against him automatically, the crown of her head sliding neatly beneath his chin as if she was the perfect fit for him. He let her go as if she were suddenly red hot and groped for a light-hearted comment to gloss over the fact that his heart rate was shimmying crazily. 'And you'll excel at the next task,' he said quickly. 'All you need to do is eat a few bugs.'

She gave him an incredulous look. He'd really got this sweet-talking thing sewn up. *Not.*

'Oh, just fantastic,' she snapped.

Why the hell had it hacked her off so much when the river thing hadn't quite gone as perfectly as she expected it to? She was amazed by how annoyed she was with herself for not being more careful with her footing. Why should she even care how it went? She hadn't expected to feel so damned triumphant when she managed to pull off the zip wire either. Despite what she might have said to Jack, did it *really* have that much to do with impressing the public?

How long had it been since she'd come across someone so enthusiastic and encouraging? She could easily see now why his survival courses had been so successful. He could instil enough trust to make you step off a ledge onto a zip wire or follow him into an icy cold swirly river, and he could make you feel great about the achievement, whether or not it had gone to plan.

She could only dream of having that confidence and charisma. Oh, she was used to having everything go her way, to people agreeing with her every whim. A trust fund did that for a person. Happen to have a family who had no real interest in you? No worries at all—with a trust fund behind you, you could buy friends, a social circle. Hell, you could buy a *life*. That was pretty much what her father had been banking on, she knew. That she would just get on with her life while he got on with his, minimal interaction necessary, his obligation to her mother fulfilled. His wallet saw to that. He'd married her mother knowing that Evie came as part of the deal, one making up for the other. When her mother had died that payoff had disappeared.

She'd learned the truth at fifteen, after he'd descended on her boarding school in response to her acting up. In anger he'd made that revelation, and her mystification and hurt at his dwindling interest in her had finally made perfect sense. He would continue to support her financially for her mother's sake but, for him, it ended there.

The desire to belong had never left her. The hope that she might still earn his love on her own terms. He was the only father she'd ever known. And there was Will, the only blood relative she had left. To him, ignorant of the facts, she was still his big sister. She'd clung to that as she tried to find her way forward after her mother's death, ashamed to tell anyone her secret for fear of losing what façade of a life she had left.

It had felt empty and inconsequential down the years. The only time she'd had a taste of anything like a sense of achievement was when she finally realised she might have enough interest through the TV show to launch her jewellery designs. A captive audience with whom she couldn't fail because the fear that she wouldn't be good enough, that she'd just sink out of sight, had made her too afraid to try before. Not when she'd sunk out of sight with her family these past twenty or so years.

Jack made failure seem somehow less scary with his gung-ho attitude about giving things a go and challenging yourself. She wanted that feeling to stay on. And that more than anything made her determined to throw herself into the eating task, one hundred per cent. It was all about impressing herself, building her confidence.

It had absolutely nothing to do, she insisted to herself, with impressing *him,* despite the growing spark she felt between them. To fall for him would go against all the safety precautions she'd built these last few years when it came to men. She already knew he only ever had flings with women—like she needed yet another one of those. A surge of nausea churned in her stomach at the thought of a liaison with Jack, this time scrutinised from wonderful start to inevitable ditch by the gleeful viewing public.

No way would she let herself be sucked into that situation again. She would keep her mind resolutely on nothing but the outdoor tasks. Jack Trent really could be a hairy hillbilly for all she cared.

CHAPTER SIX

As THEY TRUDGED downhill for forty minutes towards the final film location of the day, the camera crew clearly weren't included in the 'living off nature's bounty' thing. If Evie had to watch one more person munch their way through a chocolate bar she might be tempted to mug them.

'How much longer is this going to take?' she blurted at last, leaning against a tree with Jack while the production team organised a mocked-up table setting on a fallen log, spreading a cloth and fiddling with a cool-bag.

He glanced away from the sheet of paper he was holding, some kind of listed itinerary—goodness knew what the hell was written there.

'Shouldn't be much longer,' he said, grinning. 'Hungry, are you?'

'That's not funny. I just want it over and done with.'

A nod from the director and he led the way to the set. She approached the table reluctantly, her face already scrunching into a disgusted expression before she even saw the buffet from hell.

'Let's eat,' Jack said.

The words landed in her stomach like a rock. To one side of the table was a couple of plastic boxes, hastily removed from shot as she watched by a production minion.

'Tupperware?' she said, raising an eyebrow. 'What the hell happened to foraging nature's bounty? How exactly is *this* true to life?' It was on the tip of her tongue to ask if there was pizza.

'This is a TV show,' Jack said, stating the obvious. 'These foods are all foraged, all items it's perfectly possible to find out here. Unfortunately we're under time pressure so instead of hunting and collecting game ourselves it's been decided that we'll do a bit of a tasting demonstration.'

'Decided by who?' she asked. Clearly not Jack—his whole demeanour screamed disapproval.

'The production team,' he said, waving a hand at the handful of people. 'Naturally if you were just attending the survival course without any filming, all food would be caught by us. Obviously that can be unpredictable, very much down to what you happen to find on the day, and it can also be very time consuming. I'll explain all that to camera and we'll edit in some footage of me demonstrating how to make snares.' He paused. 'Then they thought talking through and trying a range of foods with you might add a bit more interest for the viewers.'

'I just bet they did,' she said, her temper surfacing. 'Get evil Evie to eat roasted rat and watch the hike in viewing figures—right?'

Jack shook his head.

'For the record, it wasn't my decision.' He paused for a moment as the camera clicked into action. 'You can refuse, of course. I wouldn't blame you. You're clearly used to champagne and caviar, but these are all perfectly edible foods that will keep you alive in the wild.' He turned to camera and began counting off on his fingers. 'Squirrel, rat, mealworms...' The camera zoomed in as Evie leaned over the table to look at what was on offer.

It all looked *beyond* hideous. The gnawing hunger that had resurfaced at intervals for the last couple of hours scuttled away. She was certain now that she could manage on nothing but a thimbleful of purified water for the whole weekend if necessary. When she looked up Jack's eyes were sharp with interest; he was obviously waiting to see what her reaction would be.

'If you're not up to the challenge you only have to say,' he said. He held her gaze steadily with his green eyes. 'But you can do this. Nothing on that platter will kill you.' Always the get-out opportunity. He encouraged, he didn't push.

The 'champagne and caviar' comment riled her a little. For all his impressed attitude after the river crossing, in his eyes she was clearly still nothing more than rich socialite. Purple Productions, and Jack—and undoubtedly her father and the public at large—doubted that she was up to the task. They all thought they knew her reaction before she even started. All that remained was for It-girl Evie to pull a disgusted face and make a huge on-screen fuss before tasting perhaps a corner of one of the awful chunks of 'food' and then throwing up just off-camera. That waste-of-space opinion of her would be cemented in the space of one scene of the show. Her success at the zip wire and her endurance of the river would be forgotten in the space of a few minutes as she showed her true colours after all. She decided right there that there was no way she was going to give anyone the satisfaction of seeing her fail at this. She would try every disgusting thing on offer without so much as a gag. She drew herself up to her full height.

Jack watched as she poked through the items on the table with one finger. The camera zoomed in for a close-up.

'You first,' she said.

* * *

Ten minutes later and the food had been filmed and named for the viewers, item by gruesome item, a line-up of morsels on a tin plate, some of which were—gut-churningly—moving. She locked determined eyes with Jack's amused ones and refused to drop her gaze first.

Start as you mean to go on.

She watched Jack chat to camera about the nutritional qualities of insects and grubs, many of which were apparently safely edible by humans, none of which mattered to her one bit because they looked so utterly, utterly repellent.

He made his point by picking up a couple of wormy things from the writhing mass on the plate and calmly eating them with an expression that wouldn't have looked out of place if they'd been canapés at a swanky cocktail party. He kept his eyes locked on her the entire time. She could feel her cheeks trying to pull themselves into a grimace.

'Your turn,' he said. 'Make sure you chew before you swallow them.'

Her stomach gave a sickening roll in response and she slapped him on the arm.

He laughed good-naturedly while she dug her nail extensions into her palms.

She thought of the *Miss K* fan base, expecting her to throw a hissy fit of monumental proportions before possibly resorting to tears. Was that really how she wanted to be viewed? Most of all she thought of her father with his view that all she ever did was show herself up.

'Cheese on toast,' she chanted aloud, deliberately not plumping for champagne and caviar, reaching for the plate before she could change her mind. The grubs felt vaguely squelchy beneath her fingers. 'Cheese on toast, cheese on toast.' She tried to picture the delicious crunch of toasted bread and the strong flavour of cheese, with maybe just a dash of black pepper, all the while attempting to chew without letting the grubs make contact with any part of her mouth except her teeth. Jack's eyes widened at the mad chomping. A dark and bitter-tasting stringiness flooded her mouth in spite of her efforts and by sheer will she somehow managed not to gag as she swallowed.

Then it was done; it was gone. One down, more to go. And as she looked up Jack gave her an impressed grin and a thumbs up of encouragement. She somehow felt better about herself in that moment, after eating bugs, than she had done since this whole nightmare had begun.

Within twenty minutes she'd tried everything on the plate. Including but not limited to star-of-the-show roasted rat. The sense of satisfaction she felt at not having thrown in the towel was completely unfamiliar. The camera crew moved around them, packing up equipment, ready to move to their pick-up point. One cameraman would continue with them to film them setting up camp before he departed too. Then tomorrow there were more promised outdoor sequences to be filmed. She felt oddly more on edge at the prospect of spending the night alone here, just herself and Jack, than she did at whatever might be thrown at her tomorrow. She forced herself to get a grip. She'd got through this day unscathed. How hard could it be?

'Three out of three,' Jack said, finally setting his pack down in a new clearing. Their final campsite was chosen, as he had informed the camera, because it was well sheltered and near but not too near a stream. 'Not bad. You've really held your own.'

'Really,' she said, not sure whether that could be construed as entirely complimentary when his voice was laced with surprise.

'Grown men have puked,' he said.

Unbelievable the spike of pride that caused. She wondered what that said about the lack of achievement in her life thus far. Perhaps best not to analyse that one too much.

An hour or so later and the camera had finished a run of footage covering the best place for a fire, how to collect and purify stream water, and how best to shelter if necessary. The cameraman packed up his kit and left them nerve-tinglingly alone together. The tense reality of being alone with her smacked Jack between the eyes almost immediately.

He couldn't deny he was impressed. *Surprised* and impressed. Agreeing to attend the course and actually throwing yourself into the tasks involved were two different things. She was game. He hadn't expected that. And taking part in the tasks with her was actually fun. It was all a bit of a change from the usual overenthusiastic attendees his courses attracted. Most of his candidates were only too happy to follow orders, eager to learn and impressed by his reputation. Since the TV show he could add starstruck to that mix, something which made him extremely uncomfortable.

Evie displayed none of those traits. Without an interest in survival skills or bush craft, she instead chatted to him about her childhood camping holidays and asked him about his background. As a workaholic who deliberately avoided any relationship that demanded emotional investment from him, being with someone who was interested in *chatting* to him wasn't what he was used to. Yes, there had been dates, but they were little more than photo opportunities for the press. There had been plenty of short flings when he was on leave from the army but that was years ago now, back when he was in the mind-set of taking no responsibility for anyone but himself.

On top of all that, she was much nicer to look at than the usual people who came on these things. He'd never imagined anyone could possibly look that cute with mud on their face. She was a confusing mass of behaviours. The girl he'd seen on the TV who'd tried to schmooze him onside back in the hotel for an easy life, and the girl who was determined to go through with the worst of the outdoor challenges his courses offered. So which was she?

'Thanks.' She leaned her backpack against a handy tree. 'If you wanted to stop with the "rich girl" references any time soon, that would be really good.'

He stopped what he was doing and looked at her questioningly.

'Champagne and caviar?' she said, eyebrows raised.

A smile kicked in. He'd been running with stereotype so long that it hadn't occurred to him that he might be offending her.

'Sorry.' He stood up. 'That is your life though, isn't it? Party-girl socialite. Your whole TV show buys into that.'

She dropped her eyes away, as if she disliked that comment. Silence ensued as she pawed through her own backpack and he felt a twist of regret, closely followed by exasperation. What was he doing now, analysing her every comment and reaction? He focused on the task at hand and waved a hand around at the wooded surround-ings. 'We need to get started collecting some wood, then we can get a fire up and running.' Being alone with her brought a twist of tension that it shouldn't. An evening stretching ahead, just the two of them. He swept the thought to one side. It was one night. Another campout in a long line of millions of them. *Loads* of practical tasks to deal with. He was simply knocked sideways a little by the fact that he'd started the day unimpressed by her and she'd managed to turn that opinion around. She wasn't quite what she'd seemed, back in that production meeting. That didn't happen to him often.

To prove to himself that he wasn't distracted he moved around the clearing, showing her the kind of wood that worked best. She dutifully began collecting, making a pile. Again, no sign of the diva when the camera wasn't switched on.

'What kind of things did you get up to, then, camping out as a kid?' he asked, carefully keeping the conversation on task too.

She glanced up from the pile of wood.

'Certainly nothing as full-on as eating bugs,' she said. 'Although I'm sure Will would have been up for it. Sleeping in a tent, a bit of fishing, cooking over a campfire. All the usual stuff.'

'He should be impressed, then.'

'Will?' She uttered a light laugh. 'He won't be watching. He's out on tour in the Middle East.' She shrugged wryly. 'He probably wouldn't be watching even if he was back here. My family aren't big fans of my TV appearances.' She glanced his way. 'No offence. My father actually likes *your* show. When I'm not in it at least. He thinks my TV stuff is a family embarrassment.'

He was surprised. He'd read enough about her to know she came from a hugely successful family. He'd assumed that kind of background, with a family business and a family name, automatically meant they would be close. What the hell was there to go wrong when everyone had enough money to fix any problem, no matter how large?

'I guess I assumed you had this big supportive family background,' he said. He thought of Helen, managing back at home with his mother on minimal money for months at a time when he'd been abroad. Just like Evie's brother Will, he'd never given his sister a second thought while he was away. Out of sight, out of mind. His stomach gave a guilty churn.

'Why? Because I had a privileged upbringing?' She shook her head. 'I'm not close to my family. Except for Will, when he's here, which isn't often now. The only thing holding us all together is family obligations and money.'

Her voice was oddly detached.

'You're not close, then, you and your brother?' he said, keeping his voice neutral. He concentrated on stripping the bark from a few drier branches so they would catch fire easily.

She added more sticks to the pile and sat down cross-legged to watch him.

'We were very close as kids. I'm only a year or so older so we're very close in age. I wanted to do everything he did, boys' stuff, you know. All the time, not just when we were on holidays. I was a right pest.' She paused. 'Will was always closer to my father than I was. Then after my mother died we were sent to separate boarding schools. Will headed off into the military like my father and my uncles. He fitted right in. Sometimes I envy him that. He knew what was expected of him. Role model and career path, all mapped out. I never really had any sense of direction like that.' She shrugged. 'Not until the TV stuff anyway, and that was never something I aspired to. It just came out of the blue.'

'I'm sorry about your mum,' he said.

'It was a long time ago now.'

She dashed off a brief smile and went straight back to sorting through the pile of wood. He watched her as she chose a stick and began picking at some loose bark, felt a pang of sympathy for her. Not that he'd had both parents on hand for a cushy perfect upbringing, but what you never had you never missed. His father had barely been on the scene, only resurfacing now and then to persuade his mother to give him another chance, none of which had ever lasted. One such encounter had resulted in Helen. For Jack there was no before or after to compare, just years of his mother holding it all together, working two or three jobs.

'What about you?' she asked. 'What are your family like?'

He paused for a moment. Small talk about family background wasn't a regular fixture on his camping trips. Candidates came for team building, to learn new skills and find themselves. They weren't interested in asking him personal questions. Maybe, now he thought about it, that was part of the appeal.

'I grew up with my mum and sister,' he said shortly. 'My father was never really around.' He wondered for a moment how Helen had felt when he'd been away in the army. Had she told people they weren't close? Had she felt that he wasn't interested or bothered about her?

'It's easy to get cut off from family when you're away on tour,' he said. 'The army becomes like this replacement family. You come back home and people have changed, life has shifted without you.' He paused, not sure if he was trying to justify himself to Evie or make himself feel better. 'I wish I'd stayed in touch more,' he said.

She smiled at him as he arranged the sticks ready to light a fire.

'You're back now though—right?' she said. 'Back to normal, properly in touch.'

'I'm back now, yeah.'

He didn't elaborate on just how disastrously life had shifted for Helen when his eye was off the ball.

'And, of course, you have your own lives whether you're living close or on different continents,' she carried on, clearly just running with thoughts as they entered her head. As someone who was cautious about giving literally anything of himself away, that non-filtered conversation was unfamiliar. 'However close—or not—your family might be, you have to take responsibility for your own life, pick yourself back up after mistakes, make your own way. I think it's good to count on yourself. I've got no desire to be babysat through my life or kept under someone's thumb.' She sighed, almost to herself. 'I wish someone would tell my father that.'

Jack dug in his backpack for matches in silence. There was an almost imperceptible lightening of the heavy brick of guilt that he seemed to constantly drag around with him. It was as if she'd unknowingly chipped a corner of it off with her mad desire for independence parroting Helen's recent gerroff-my-back complaints at his overprotectiveness. Never mind that Evie and Will were from a different world from him and Helen. They were still brother and sister with the same army distance between them, the same challenges. It was hard. Letting someone make and recover from their own mistakes was hard when they were the kind of mistakes Helen made.

'Can we light the fire?'

Her face was eager and his heart turned over softly before he could get a grip. She made him feel better about himself. Not astoundingly so; there was no bolt of lightning in which he suddenly felt at ease. He wasn't sure he'd ever be capable of that—of a sudden exoneration from blaming himself. It was more a tiny loosening of tension, so gradual that he barely picked up on it, but there just the same. It had been a long time since anyone had done that.

Jack handed her the pack of matches and Evie scratched one and held it against the bark until the flame ate its way to the tips of her fingers. The flames grew easily and she caught herself kneeling opposite Jack and beaming with excitement. For Pete's sake, less than a day in wind and rain with no Internet access and she'd reverted to someone who was impressed by a bloody *fire*. What had he done to her?

Ten minutes later and Jack had fed the fire into a steady burn.

'I wondered why you hadn't turned up at the hotel with a gang of hangers-on,' he said, watching the flames. 'I'd expected a team of people and it turned out to just be you.'

'My entourage?' she said with a smile. 'That's actually quite funny. My father's reaction to the whole thing was to offer to spirit me out of the country until the media fuss died down. He was hardly going to come and cheer me on when I went ahead with this show.' She pointed at him with a stick. 'Not that he's ever cheered me on at anything really. He's so hideously convinced that I'll never get through the weekend, no way was I going to give him the satisfaction.'

She thought of her father's angry phone call the night before she'd left for Scotland. His fury had been at such dizzying levels she could almost feel his apoplexy over the phone and it brought another sickening surge of resentment. His words resounded in her mind:

You haven't a hope in hell of completing a survival skills course. There's no point arguing with me, Evangeline, you simply don't have it in you. You'll make an even bigger fool of yourself than you already have. Just drop the plan right now. You can stay in the house in France until the whole thing blows over.'

'This is the first time in my life that I've really taken control,' she said. 'With the TV show, I mean. My father's been in charge of everything since I was just a kid. The school I went to, what I did during the holidays, where I live, the people I mix with. He supports me financially so he sees that as his right. He called me before I left for Scotland and it was the most rattled he's been since I was suspended from school for causing an explosion in the science lab.'

She glanced up to see him grin at that.

'He wanted me to go and stay at our house in the South of France, out of the country and swept under the carpet until he decides this whole mess has blown over. Until I behave. Basically he wanted to hide me away where my family don't need to think about me. Cracks nicely papered over.'

Sticking out this weekend was the only way she had of putting things right, of regaining that great few months when all was going well, when viewing figures were climbing and she was in demand for TV appearances and magazine shoots, when the public were friendly, when she had some independence and felt worth something for once.

'I said no,' she said. 'Obviously. There was no way

he was going to come and cheer me on after that. And Will is away.'

'What about friends?'

'The people I socialise with are mainly to do with the TV show. They weren't really keen on leaving London for the Highlands. So I came on my own.'

He stood up and walked the short distance to the stream to fill a pot with water.

Her background wasn't exactly the cushy number he'd taken it for. Oh, there was money there, of course, but it sounded as if she had no one in her life that really cared for her. He wondered what the deal was between her and her father. There was obviously no love lost there.

'Have a look through my rucksack—there should be a pack of rice in there,' he called back to her. 'We'll cook up some rations.'

She got up onto her knees and began rummaging.

'You really know how to plan a meal,' she said. 'Bugs for dinner, rice for supper.'

'And all the time you could be relaxing in the South of France.' He grinned, coming back. He moved the pot into place on the fire and tipped in some rice. 'Seriously, I don't get it,' he said, sitting back down on the opposite side of the fire. 'You had the choice of a sunshine holiday or doing this TV show with me. Not that I'm complaining. I'm glad you're here.'

'You are?'

His heart gave a sudden jump as he looked up to see her watching him, clear eyed, through the woodsmoke.

'If this show hadn't gone ahead my kids' initiative would have been in serious trouble,' he qualified quickly.

'Right.' She dropped her eyes. What else had she expected him to say? His pulse kept up the speed.

'At the time you agreed to do this thing at that crazy meeting in London, you didn't have a clue about the charity side of my work but you were determined to go ahead with it anyway.' He stirred the rice with a wooden spoon. 'So what I'm saying is, are you really that fame-crazed that you'll do anything at all to keep the limelight?' he said, his brows knitting in a puzzled frown. 'Is that what this is about? Keeping yourself in the public eye?'

The more he thought about it, the more the situation just didn't seem to add up. She didn't come across as a publicity animal at all; she was nothing like the girl he'd seen on the few clips of *Miss Knightsbridge* that he'd been able to stomach and the lack of designer clothes and gloss had nothing to do with it. He had no idea what the real story was with her.

'It's not about being fame-crazed—that's just a side-effect,' she said quietly.

He truly thought that was all she was after, then—headline chasing. She'd bigged up that persona to the country at large and now they all thought of her as shallow. Worst of all, *he* thought that, despite all the encouragement and challenge of the day. It made her stomach churn miserably. Somewhere along the way she'd come to like him despite all the gruff outdoorsy stuff, and now she *cared* what he thought of her. As if she needed that.

He was looking at her with interest and she turned away, unfastening her sleeping bag from her pack, and the mat that would underlie it. Finding a flat spot with no tree roots and stones was going to be a bit of a challenge. Only tonight to get through. She had no need to discuss this with him; a quick fob-off would surely be enough. There must be hundreds of things they could talk about. If she just got him started on outward-bound stuff he must have hundreds of gut-churning, all-weather endurance anecdotes to take them into the night.

'I do have a wealthy background but that girl on TV really isn't me,' she said, before she could overthink it, not looking at him. 'It's complicated.'

Jack could see just from the way she was fiddling with the sleeping bag and kit that she was uncomfortable. Now she was pawing more stuff from her backpack, sorting through it. Why the stressing?

'In what way?' he pressed.

There was a pause long enough for him to assume that was all he would get, and then unexpectedly, 'Can you keep a secret?' she said at last.

Their eyes met across the crackling fire. Her blue gaze was cautious and he tried for a joke. At her expense unfortunately.

'You're asking *me* that?' he said. 'After your loose-lipped cock-up in that restaurant?'

She threw her hands up.

'For goodness' sake, do we have to cover that again? How many times do I have to apologise? Just forget I said anything. Let's just get on with the cooking.'

He held up his hands.

'OK, OK, I'm sorry. Bad joke. Yes, I can keep a secret.'

She narrowed her eyes in a very cute sceptical expression as if she was trying to read his mind. His pulse gave a jolt in response.

'I *can*,' he repeated. 'What happens in the Highlands stays in the Highlands. You have my word.'

She paused a moment longer. Bloody hell, was she going to ask him to sign in blood?

She took a deep breath.

'The TV It-girl thing is just a front,' she said. 'I'm nothing like her at all. It's a fit-up.'

CHAPTER SEVEN

THERE WAS A moment's pause as she waited for him to process that, still wondering if she was crazy for telling him. Why the hell would he care that she had a TV image? Except that he hadn't been impressed for a single moment by diva Evie. Quite the opposite, in fact. He'd been far nicer to her since she was scrubbed of makeup, in hideous clothes and probably smelling awful too. Supportive and encouraging. It had been lovely to be herself for once without feeling invisible. Even if it was just for the weekend with a man she'd never see again.

'I don't understand. You do have that background, right?' he said, his expression puzzled. 'You're *that* Staverton-Lynch. I read up on it. Your family is one of the oldest in the country. They made their millions from property.'

The familiar surge of unease kicked in, as if he somehow knew how tenuous her link to that family really was, which of course he couldn't possibly. No one knew. She tried to act normal and gloss over it. What the hell else could she do? She could hardly say, *Actually, I'm not that Staverton-Lynch. I'm an imposter, and if it weren't for Will I'd have no link to that family at all.* As far as she was aware no one knew her secret. Even Will. For all appearances she was the eldest child of John Staverton-Lynch. That was the way her father wanted it, and without an identity or alternative life of her own she was too scared to do anything but go along with his wishes.

She felt an odd sense of embarrassment about her no-expenses-spared background, as if it weren't public knowledge. He must think she'd sailed through life on a cushion of wealth while he'd grafted his way up and there was the usual assumption that the money had somehow made that life a breeze. *He'd been reading about her.* Her pulse quickened a little at that and she shook her head lightly. What did she care if he'd showed an interest in her background? It didn't mean anything. It wasn't as if he had to look very hard; it was probably rehashed in every current newspaper.

'Yes, I am that Staverton-Lynch, as you call it,' she said. 'But I'm not really anything like the girl you see on TV. It's an image, built up for the show. The public think I'm some headline-grabbing, fame-crazed diva who hangs out in glitzy nightspots and acts like a spoilt brat in shops.'

He stared at her until the rice pot made an attempt to boil over. He leaned in quickly to stir it and shook his head slowly.

'Forgive me if I'm missing the point, but if you're not like that, and you have the wealthy background, why the hell are you doing that ludicrous *Miss Knightsbridge* show at all?' He stirred the rice vigorously. She could almost see his mind working. 'You don't need the money and now you're telling me the rich diva lifestyle isn't your thing. So that means—what—it really is all about *fame* for you?'

His expression was mystified. And no wonder. It sounded ludicrous, even to her.

'No, it's not about the fame! It never has been. I just

kind of *fell* into it and before I knew where I was this whole persona had been built up.' She picked up one of the sticks from the woodpile and peeled at a piece of loose bark. 'The thing was that when the show took off it opened up a whole lot of new options for me. *That's* what it's really about. I know Roasted Ratgate hasn't exactly been a picnic for you—' she pointed at him with the stick '—but I really shot myself in the foot with that comment. There's a lot more riding on the show for me than fame.'

'What do you mean?'

'You've built your business up on the back of your show, haven't you?' she said. It was something she couldn't help admiring about him, that he'd seized the opportunity that had fallen into his lap and made something real from it. Something more than the fake public interest, hell, the fake *life* that she'd managed. 'Well, I'm hoping to do the same.'

She chanced a look up at him through her eyelashes, her heart suspended mid-beat as she waited for an expected reaction to match her father's. His expression was one of interested surprise. No negativity that she could see. She looked down again quickly before she bottled out of telling him.

'When all this stuff kicked off I was just about to launch my own business, something serious that I'd been too afraid to do for years.' She took a breath. 'I make jewellery. Silver mostly. I did a course a long time ago and I've been developing designs ever since.' She smiled to herself. 'For a long time it was doubtful any of it would get beyond my living room. I made gifts for friends, that kind of thing, and I made things for myself, but I was way too scared of going further than that. And then a couple of viewers contacted the TV show, asking where they could buy a dress ring I'd worn.'

The excitement she'd felt at that moment bubbled back through her. She couldn't imagine that feeling ever getting old—the sensation that someone liked her designs without knowing their origin. Liking her for her own talent or ability, unfettered by prejudice at the kind of person she might or might not be, without reference to her family ties or lack of them.

'I realised I could use the show as a springboard to launch my designs commercially,' she said. 'I'd been so afraid of the whole thing tanking that I'm not sure I'd ever have dared go ahead with it if it wasn't for the TV show. I realised that if I linked my jewellery brand to the show there was less risk of screwing up because I had a captive market. I would be making my own money. I thought I could prove my father wrong for once.' She paused. 'He thinks I'm good for nothing.'

He pulled the pot of rice to one side of the fire, not speaking. What had she expected? He probably thought she was insane. Hell, it sounded insane spoken out loud. With Jack's proper respectable business and charity work his own TV image was a sideline. He already had his own successful life outside it all.

'It sounds fantastic,' he said.

She glanced sharply at him, so stiff and detached, like her father. Had he actually used the word 'fantastic'? She hadn't realised how certain she was of a negative reaction from him. 'Can't do.' Just like her father on the telephone.

'Really?' she said. For Pete's sake, her voice sounded pathetically grateful. She cleared her throat and tried again. 'You think it does?'

He nodded.

'Absolutely. My sister mentioned your jewellery. Some butterfly necklace you wore the other week— she liked it and wanted to know where you got it. I don't suppose that was one of yours?'

She realised she was staring at him.

'Yes!' she said excitedly. 'I made it. She seriously liked it? You can't imagine how lovely that is for me. I'll make one for her.'

'She'd love that. I'll pay for it, of course.'

She flapped a hand at him.

'Don't be daft. I wouldn't dream of it.'

He was watching her quietly, his expression hard to fathom. She wondered vaguely if she'd offended him, as if she could splash the cash as necessary and that dashing off a necklace for his sister meant nothing when it actually made her want to jump around the camp with pride.

'I'd like to,' she said. 'As a thank you for getting me through the weekend.'

'You're not through it yet,' he pointed out, but he was grinning now and she was relieved. 'That's nice of you. The business sounds great. It's obviously got appeal in the eighteen-year-old girl bracket, judging by Helen's reaction. Not that I know much about jewellery, but everyone needs a sense of direction. I'm all for work. I've seen what can happen when people have no sense of purpose, what it does to your self-esteem. I'm sure you'll do brilliantly. Don't let anyone stand in your way.'

Before she could stop herself her excitement at his enthusiasm bubbled over and she walked around the fire on her knees, a broad grin on her face. He jumped a little as she leaned in and kissed his mud-gritted cheek on impulse.

'Thank you,' she said.

A surprised grin touched his mouth as she shifted on her knees back around the fire to her own bedroll.

'You're very welcome.'

She sat down cross-legged and looked into the fire, unable to keep the smile off her face.

'So just to clarify,' he said, 'the diva the-world-is-ending reaction to the mud on the face was all an act. For the cameras, so to speak.'

There was amusement in the green eyes as they met hers.

She blew a stray tendril of hair off her face.

'Don't get me wrong—I think you'd be hard pressed to find any girl who'd let herself be filmed caked in mud without putting up some kind of protest. But yes.' She shrugged. 'I guess it was. You saw the public backlash in the press. They want to see me humiliated on screen, not enjoying it all like a happy camper. I was just giving what I thought they wanted.'

'And the we-understand-one-another schmoozing back in your hotel room to get some kind of easy ride?'

She shrugged.

'I was public enemy number one. I thought it couldn't hurt to get you onside a bit.'

'And as the day's gone on—'

'I kind of lost sight of playing that part. The stupid tasks were hard enough without having to stay in some kind of mad It-girl character. It was a relief, if I'm honest, to just be myself for once.'

He opened his mouth to speak and she stopped him with a held-up hand before he got the wrong idea and suggested they up the perceived enjoyment level by bringing in cave-diving or something equally terrifying.

'Before you get carried away, I'm not a secret fan of the great outdoors. Believe it or not, I would rather be curled up at home with a box set than sleeping in the forest.' She looked down at her hands. 'But I'm not really a party girl either. Or a shopping addict. Those are a means to an end. And now I've told you I really ought to kill you.'

She waited, staring down at her hands for him to respond. Just what kind of idiot would he think she was now? When all she got was silence she glanced up to test the look on his face.

He was smiling across at her, that gorgeous smile that floored the nation's women. Except she was the only one here and it was just for her.

'Your secret's safe with me,' he said. 'No need for violence.'

He held her eyes a beat too long and her stomach softened deliciously. She knew flirting when she heard it and that last comment definitely smacked of it. As she cut her own eyes away they took in the shapeless jacket and trousers combo she was wearing. She hadn't a scrap of make-up on and she couldn't begin to even imagine what kind of bird's nest her hair must look like. She'd seen the kind of women Jack Trent went for and she hadn't seen a single one that channelled the dragged-through-a-hedge look.

Scratch that about flirting. Far more likely that comment was a sympathy boost.

Jack built up the fire and she'd unrolled her sleeping bag and shoved her legs inside it. Past dusk now, the wood full of sounds that hadn't registered with her in the daytime. The crackling rustle of small animals moving around, the wind rippling through the treetops, the crackle and spit of the fire. It cast a glow for a short distance and beyond the darkness was impenetrably perfect.

The smell of woodsmoke drifted on the air. She sat as close to the fire as she could without her sleeping bag catching fire. Jack's stomach was a knot of tension. At the night in the wilderness, he insisted to himself, not at being alone with her.

It all made a kind of sense to Jack now. The glimpses of likeable among the spoilt behaviour since she'd arrived here. She'd started out in the London production meeting channelling full-on socialite princess, and then the more he got to know her and the further she got from that comfort zone, the more he began to see a normal, fun young woman with hang-ups like everyone else and a very obvious aversion to failing or giving up, which he could relate to one hundred per cent.

Without being thrown together by the show he'd never have got to know her, any more than he put himself in a position to get to know anyone. And he liked her. He liked the way she looked, he liked her backchat, he liked her determination and optimism in the face of what sounded like constant discouragement from her family. Why deny it? Why not let himself enjoy her company for one evening? It couldn't hurt. This time tomorrow they'd be back at the hotel and he'd most likely never see her again.

That thought really shouldn't be the downer that it seemed to be.

'It does makes a certain kind of sense,' he said, settling down opposite. 'The whole TV image thing. At the beginning I thought you were going to complain your way through every task. The TV crew were geared up for monumental tantrums. I never thought you'd make it to the end.'

'I know you didn't,' she said. The look in her blue eyes was of pure satisfaction and that spark of attraction kicked right back in at her triumphant vibe. The boost he always got from watching people outdo themselves on his courses.

'Really?'

He looked at her questioningly because he prided himself on his ability to make his course candidates feel positive, to lead by encouragement.

'Champagne and caviar?' she reminded him. 'The suggestion that any camping holiday I might have would be a luxury one? Be honest, you thought I wasn't up to this thing right from the start.'

He inclined his head slightly. She'd earned it.

'Point taken,' he said. She'd been on the back foot with him from the outset after the media fiasco. He supposed he'd let that prejudice seep into some of his comments. He wasn't quite as professional as he hoped he was.

'I'm not sure I actually need any of that,' Evie said, nodding at the pot on the fire filled with rice from Jack's rations and her own. 'I'm still full from the *delicious* meal you served to me earlier.'

He grinned.

'Just think how it will make you appreciate food more when you get back to reality.'

She prodded the fire with a stick. It was hypnotic; there was something cosy about watching the flames dance. He sat cross-legged on his bedroll on the other side of the flames.

'*This* is reality for you though, isn't it?' she said. 'With your TV show it's what-you-see-is-what-you-get. The real me is far too boring to make good viewing. To-night Evie Staverton-Lynch tries out a new brand of luxury hot chocolate while watching TV in her onesie.' She grinned. '*Miss Knightsbridge* would have been dropped after one episode.'

'How on earth did you get on the show if you're nothing like the character they wanted?'

'That's a funny story,' she said.

'I'm listening.'

She wriggled a little further into her sleeping bag and took a metal mug of boiled rice from him. She took a tiny spoonful. Bland and gelatinous, but delicious compared to the ghastly food task.

'I was living in London not long after I finished college and I went to a birthday party at the last minute. One of my old school friends—I hadn't seen her for years.' She took another taste of the rice. 'My father hadn't been in touch for ages, except for the usual messages from his PA, and then suddenly he was there with his date.'

'A date?'

'My mother died when I was twelve,' she said. 'Since then he has a couple of old family friends who go to these things with him. No romance involved as far as I know. Not since my mum died.'

His face was carefully neutral.

'It can't have been easy, losing your mum like that.'

No pause to respond to that; she simply breezed ahead. She'd been breezing ahead for years. It had become her coping strategy.

'Maybe he couldn't cope with the reminders of her. He just shut down where I was concerned, pretty much from the moment she died, not that we were ever really close.' She toyed with the mug of rice, thinking back. On some level the revelation that she wasn't his child at all had come as a relief. At least she had a *reason* now for his cold and deliberate detachment from her, instead of those early years of miserable confusion and abandonment. 'He's your typical stiff-upper-lip military man. No way of telling what he's thinking. Impossible to read.' She glanced his way. 'I thought at first you might be like that too, but I was wrong.

'No offence,' she added quickly as he raised an eyebrow. She took a deep breath, sweeping on. 'He likes me best when I'm away somewhere, like school or college, kept busy. Kept quiet. I'm a pain in the arse of a loose end. At school I used to act up just to make that difficult for him.'

She wrapped her hands around the tin mug to warm them.

'My father wasn't exactly delighted to see me at this party.' She shrugged. *'Awkward.* It was like school all over again. I was so determined to show him what a great time I was having, I drank far too much, knocked over a table and eventually got removed from the party. He left with his escort on his arm and I woke up with the mother of all hangovers the next day. I don't really drink, you see.'

He nodded.

'Next thing I know, I get a call from Purple Productions, briefing me on this new reality show they've come up with. The whole concept of fly-on-the-wall had really taken off and one of their team had been at the party. They assumed behaving like a diva in public was par for the course with me. Then they found out my background and that was it. Apparently I was exactly what they were looking for—rich socialite behaving badly with old-school family living in swanky West London on her trust fund. Except that I was never really like that at all.'

'If the trust fund fits,' he said.

She laughed at that. It really was funny.

'Exactly. People just see money and think everything must be easy.'

The money and the name was all she had left of her life.

'At the beginning I took it on thinking it would annoy my father.' Desperation to retain a shred of her father's attention had led her to try anything, fuelled by the irrational feeling that as long as he didn't stop noticing her she could still have a part of his life. 'I never expected it to take off the way it did. I got myself an agent, Chester, and he's the one who built up the whole It-girl image. He gets the magazine shoots and interviews, that kind of thing. Then I started to make a bit of money for myself, and that felt great after so many years of going cap in hand to my father if I wanted anything, feeling reliant on him for everything. It's only recently that I've started to see I could use the show as a springboard to finally start my own business. I finally started to believe I had a direction at last, something for *me*.'

He looked at her intently across the fire as he finished the last few spoons of his own rice. An unexpected pang of sympathy coursed through him. That fall-back position of hers was most people's dream. It had been so easy to simply imagine her with enough money to buy whatever she wanted and generations of rich and supportive family behind her, that he'd assumed happiness came along as part of the package. Losing your mother so young was awful. Her father sounded useless. Maybe money made that easier on a practical level but it couldn't change the fact that she was basically on her own.

'What about you?' she said, pointing at him with her

spoon. 'What's your family like? Are they all mad for the great outdoors too?'

He shook his head at the ludicrousness of that idea.

'You probably spent more time outdoors as a kid than I did with your camping holidays. We lived in London, inner city. One of those grey concrete blocks of flats on an estate. The kind of estate where you feel like you're entering a whole different universe when you go there.'

He doubted she'd ever been within shouting distance of such a place.

'You probably haven't a clue what that would be like,' he said. 'It has the obligatory row of shops, one of which is a twenty-four-hour grocery store. Kids hang around on corners. There's always a playground and it's always covered in graffiti and half the equipment is broken. Everyone knows everyone else and whole branches of families live within walking distance of each other. The police look there first if there's a drug bust.'

She was staring at him. He checked himself. His inner hatred of the place and what it had done to his family had never really gone away.

'Is that why you joined the army?' she said. 'To get away?'

He looked away.

'Something like that, yeah. I joined at nineteen. Things weren't going too well for me at home at the time.'

A light gloss over the full story. The usual grip of shame held his tongue when it came to revisiting his past behaviour.

'Before I met you I thought maybe you had family in the forces like me. Your father perhaps. Then you told me he wasn't really on the scene.'

He failed to stop a sarcastic smile at that. Dusk was

kicking in now but in the light from the fire she didn't miss it.

'What's funny?' She smiled back questioningly.

'The idea that my father would have the nous to join the forces. Too much like hard work. Come to think of it, anything is too much like hard work for him.' He glanced at her. 'Your father is at least *interested* in what you're doing, even if it comes across as criticism. I haven't heard from mine for years. Which means my TV stuff has completely passed him by because, trust me, he would have been in touch by now if he'd sniffed money. He's either dead, out of the country or off his head so much of the time that he's not living in the real world.'

That deep inner thought surfaced, the way it always did when he thought of his father. He had escaped to the army, deserting his family as surely as his father had done before him, leaving them to whatever might come. With it came the niggling fear: could that be him again in the future if the situation were right, walking away from those he needed?

A prickling sense of shame made Evie's cheeks feel suddenly a little warm at the thought of all the moaning she'd done about her father. Jack's background sounded hideous.

'So it was just you and your mother growing up?' she said.

The old curiosity gnawed at her deep inside as she asked the question. What was it like to grow up, all the way up, with a mum? She imagined her own mother would have been the perfect warm, loving, go-to protector with whom she could have shared everything. She had that luxury. She could make her mother whatever she wanted her to be, in her mind.

'And Helen,' he said. He smiled as he said his sister's name. Evie liked that.

'Older or younger?'

'Eight years younger,' Jack said. 'My father left us for the last time while my mother was pregnant with Helen, and from then on it really was just the three of us. Before that he'd still pitch up now and then, when whoever he'd hooked up with had thrown him out. When he had something to gain from it. After the first few times I quit thinking he'd stay. A few more times and I realised it wasn't me he came back for at all.'

Evie's mind worked overtime. What would Jack say if he knew her own real father had walked away before she was born, just like his? They had more in common than he could possibly know. Except that Jack hadn't had a rich replacement to step into his father's shoes. And Jack had taken control of his own life in a way that she could only dream of.

'He makes my father sound like parent of the year,' she said. 'And all I've done is whinge about him.'

He shrugged it off.

'I think Helen had it worse than I did. It took its toll on her, that he never showed an interest in even knowing her.'

He stared into the fire, his expression distant. The silence was bordering on long enough to kill the conversation and she realised she didn't want that. For all its hard-floored, no-shower lack of luxury, she suddenly didn't want the evening to end. When had she last got to know a man beyond surface impressions? The men she dated never confided in her like this. For them it really had been skin deep.

'What about girlfriends?' She broke the silence. 'The papers are full of your dates.'

He met her eyes, held them steadily. Tension clung in the air like the woodsmoke—her fault; she was the one who'd tipped the conversation towards his love-life. Her heart picked up the pace. She could feel it clattering madly in her chest.

'Exactly,' he said. '*Dates.* No one special. I spent a long time away in the army, then some of the expeditions I've done have been for months at a time. Romance doesn't really fit with all of that. I've worked too hard on my business to get distracted by relationships now that it's finally up and running.' His tone was measured, making her wonder if there was more to it than that. He took a sip of water. 'You're the first girl I've taken alone on one of these trips.'

'Really?'

Butterflies were kicking off in her stomach at the intense way he watched her through the curls of smoke from the fire. She'd assumed from all the press stories that he was a real charmer, bored with a girl after a couple of dates, always moving on. The kind of man she'd made so many mistakes with. It turned out he wasn't like that after all, he was simply too committed to his work, he was focused on his family, both traits that she couldn't help being drawn to. And now he was saying she was different? Her heart was clattering as if she'd run a dozen circuits of the camp.

He nodded. 'Sometimes get women coming along as part of a group but I don't really do one-to-one survival excursions. I've had a couple of people guest on the show before, similar format to this, but never a woman. Not until you. It works better really with more people, get them working as part of a team. You're something of a special case.'

Her pulse was jumping up in bounds. Just bloody

great, a night alone with Jack Trent and she'd morphed into a stupid teenager.

'Good special or nightmare special?'

He caught her gaze in his.

'Both.'

CHAPTER EIGHT

SETTLING DOWN TO sleep felt out of the question and he usually slept like a baby outdoors. Did she know he was watching her pull her blonde hair free, rake her fingers through it and tie it loosely to one side of her neck? She didn't look his way for a second. The movements drew his eyes to the smooth curve of her neck and higher to the heart-shaped face and soft mouth. Scrubbed of all make-up, one small smear of mud left high up on one cheekbone, that one flaw managing to highlight the smooth porcelain creaminess of her skin beyond anything her usual polished glossy make-up achieved. The golden glow of the firelight cast shadows on her pretty face.

They might have been the only two people in the universe and every cell in his body seemed to have heightened awareness of her and her movements around their small camp. She stood a few feet away from the fire to undress, on the edge of the glowing light it threw out, partly hidden from his view by bushes. Heat curled through his body as he caught glimpses of her removing the heavy outer coat and trousers, keeping on the figure hugging layers beneath. His pulse jumped at the flash of long slender legs as she walked quickly back to the fire and climbed into her sleeping bag and the huge erection he was sporting felt impossibly constrained by the outdoor clothing he wore. What the hell was going on with his self-control?

Then again, he reasoned madly, when did he ever spend the night in the exclusive company of someone as hot as her with an agenda that didn't include sex? Always a short-term agenda. One night, two at most. His body was simply running with the usual expectations. He set his own bed up on the opposite side of the fire. Deliberate distance. He lay down and looked across at her, lying on her side. Her eyes met his. She'd rolled up her jacket to use as a pillow. Tendrils of blonde hair curled softly around her face.

'Don't you ever get scared?' she said softly. 'Out in these places on your own?'

She was absolutely adorable. His arousal showed no signs of standing down. He swallowed hard, his mind racing.

'Not now,' he said. 'Not in this country, doing campouts like these. Army operations were different, I've spent some tense nights over the years. But that's on a mission, as part of a team. Any danger comes with the territory.' He glanced up at the canopy of tree branches. Tiny shards of silver moonlight slanted through here and there. 'You'll be safe with me,' he said.

'I know.'

That answer and the way she held his eyes raised another surge of heat through his lower body.

'There are no proper predators here,' he said, latching onto the subject. It was becoming harder by the minute to keep himself on task. 'Much worse in South America. Spiders, snakes.'

She pulled a face.

'They obviously prefer a warmer climate. Can't say

I blame them,' she said, pulling her sleeping bag more tightly around her.

'Are you cold?'

'I'm sleeping outdoors.' Her voice was lightly exasperated. 'It's May. Of course I'm bloody cold.'

Reservations and personal rules were easy to ignore when your different worlds had come together for a short couple of days. After this weekend their paths would never cross again. He knew that. It made shifting his bedroll and sleeping bag to her side of the fire seem a natural and *sensible* thing to do. He was being a gentleman. It didn't mean he was making a move; it didn't need to mean anything.

He bedded down next to her. Perfectly straightforward. Two sleeping bags between them.

'It'll be warmer if I lie here,' he said. 'Fire on that side, body heat on the other. Try and get some sleep.'

She turned slowly in her sleeping bag to face him, her face inches from his own.

'Goodnight, Jack,' she whispered.

Before he realised what she was doing she'd leaned in towards him and touched his lips softly with hers. She smelled sweetly of the baby wipes she'd smuggled along and she tasted of toothpaste, and the moment her lips were against his he had absolutely no chance.

Before she could move away he raised a hand and slid fingers into her hair, tugging it from its loose tie and relishing its silkiness, his thumbs stroking along the softness of her jaw. The silk of her skin beneath his hands was delicious, the closeness tantalisingly unfamiliar in the outdoor situation. He tilted her face gently. Another kiss, his own kiss this time, deeper, a chance to savour her.

The fire spat and popped behind her. Evie was

vaguely aware of it warming her back as his tongue slipped softly against her own. One of her hands crept up and around his neck, with the other she felt her way slowly over the padded sleeping bag to curl it around his back.

Delicious heat coursed through her as she pushed her reservations aside. Jack Trent was not some wannabe partygoer, desperate for the kudos of bedding *Miss Knightsbridge*. He had his own life, his own agenda, and he wasn't remotely seduced by shallow motivations. This was not a repeat of her same old mistake, made again and again in her desperation for love and approval. He was different. With him she could be herself, and for once that was good enough.

His hands curved around her body to pull her tightly against him. Even through the layers of wadded fabric between them the hard bulk of his body felt deliciously powerful. Leaving her mouth, he kissed her eyelids, her cheekbones, soft baby kisses that made her stomach melt as he tangled his hands in her hair. Total gentleness, unexpected from such a powerfully muscled man. Nerve endings jumped through her body, hot need peaking at her nipples and burning between her legs, and when he suddenly sat up she lay and looked up at him in the firelight, wondering if he was backing off, not wanting him to.

The darkness was a black curtain behind his head; her breath was speeding. In a couple of quick movements, he unzipped his sleeping bag and hers. A rush of cold air swept in before he zipped them back up, joining them into one cosy padded space with room for two. He lay back beside her and pulled her against him, groped for her mouth with his, found it and kissed her again.

The forest floor was firm beneath her back. He made

no attempt to undress her. Instead his hands slowly explored her, finding their way beneath the layers of clothes to reach bare skin. His palm slid over her breast and he caught the hard peak of her nipple between his fingers, tightening them until she sighed into his mouth. In response he caught her thermal top in his free hand and pushed it up until her breasts were exposed first to the cold air and then as he moved his head lower the warmth of his mouth. His lips closed over her nipple and he stroked his tongue slowly back and forth across the tip, sending sparks of hot desire through her. She wound her legs around him and tugged at his T-shirt until she found the rock-hard skin of his torso. She raked her fingers higher, over the muscled bulk of his back and shoulders. His erection was a hard pressure against her and she ground her hips instinctively against him.

The unfamiliarity of the cool outdoor air was unlike anything Evie had ever experienced. That and the fact that this was her, just her, with none of the rich trappings of her London life, and he was still interested. Sexual encounters for her had been few and far between. Relationships rarely lasted long after they'd made column inches. Wined and dined in luxury, steeped in flattery and attention which always seemed to disintegrate after the event, as if sleeping with Miss Knightsbridge was the real deal, and waking up to the day-after-day reality of boring old Evie was a disappointment. She wasn't good enough to live up to the image people had of her. She'd always fallen short.

Her sense of time seemed to dissipate out here. So far away from everything she knew, no luxuries, no soft bed. She looked like hell and she'd caused Jack nothing but trouble and yet she'd never felt so desirable. The perfect darkness around the glow of the fire made this feel like a tiny, intimate world just for them, miles and miles away from everything she knew, where anything was possible and consequences need not apply.

His hands slid lower, her mind following their progress as he tugged the band of her thermal trousers free and eased them down. A trace of ego-boosting happiness at that—she was wearing passion-killing thermal underwear and he still found her attractive! Then his fingers crept beneath the lace of her panties and pushed out all coherent thoughts, even ego-boosting ones, with an all-consuming wave of pleasure. She heard her own gasping cry as he slid two fingers inside her and found a slow, heady rhythm that drove the delicious sensation on and on. His thumb found her most sensitive spot and circled it lazily. He found her mouth again with his and kissed her hard and deep, responding to her frenzied clutching at his back by increasing his pace until she tipped over that dizzy edge of pleasure.

Jack listened to her breath even out slowly, kissed her hair as she trembled against him, and tensed as she let her hands slide lower to creep inside his clothes, freeing his huge erection. He sucked in breath as she ran soft fingertips over his length.

With a huge effort he caught her hand in his before he could lose all sense.

'What's wrong?' she said against his mouth.

He kissed her softly.

'Nothing,' he whispered. 'We can't go any further. No condoms.'

She pulled away to lean on one elbow and looked at him. The smile sparkling in her china-blue eyes made another surge of heat course through his veins.

'You mean we found something you can't make from nature's bounty?'

He laughed and she stopped his mouth with a kiss.

She gently disengaged her hand from his and went right back to that slow stroking that made it feel as if he might explode.

'We'll just have to improvise,' she said.

Jack came to as the pale tendrils of dawn began to infiltrate the heavy branches high above the forest floor. Roughly the same time as always and no slumbering about while his body took time to come round, he was fully alert from the instant he opened his eyes. Years of sleeping outdoors, often in hostile territory, had that effect on a person. Even after all that time, he was breaking new ground with this weekend.

For the first time ever on a campout, he had a half-dressed woman in his arms.

He somehow managed to remain completely motionless. Not easy while his mind was giving a smouldering run-through of highlights of the night and certain parts of his body had an agenda of their own. All the while he was acutely aware of Evie's slender body moulded to his and the softness of her blonde hair against his chest. He vaguely remembered now removing her thermal leggings at one point to reveal the smoothest, silkiest and longest legs, now curled softly around his own. At the thought heat began to rev right back up below the waist and he gritted his teeth hard and disentangled himself from her as gently and quietly as he could before he could lose his grip on the situation. She sighed in her sleep as he finally managed to creep from the sleeping bag, and he tucked it back around her before moving away to the opposite side of the fire.

Physical contact broken, his mind took over and worked overtime as he watched her sleeping in the silvery dawn light through the ribbons of smoke drifting from the embers of the fire. One hand was tucked beneath her cheek. Her golden hair was spread over the rolled-up jacket she'd used as a makeshift pillow. Last night in the darkness consequences had seemed all too distant. Now, hours too late, his mind took over from his body and ran through a list of implications.

What the hell had he done?

Last night had touched him on a level he wasn't used to. He'd been so careful not to put himself in any situation where he got to know a woman beyond the surface. Sex, when it happened, was never *meaningful*. It was about fun; it was easy to walk away from.

She was different.

Because they'd been thrown together he'd had time and space to talk to her without any romantic agenda. Far from it—at the outset he'd had every reason to be angry with her and she'd hardly been quick to channel contrite. Regard for her had crept up on him. This wasn't the usual shallow liaison and she wasn't the young woman he'd thought she was at first. She hadn't had the cushy life he'd imagined. She had her own demons, just as he did. She'd defied loss and rejection to come back fighting. She was kind; she was funny. Bloody hell, he had it bad.

She sighed softly in her sleep and he raked his hands back into his hair, thinking hard.

It was her unexpected determination to put things right that had caused all this. Her reassurance that she would go through with what amounted to trial by TV rather than leave him to sort out the mess she'd made of his reputation. He couldn't help admiring that. Add in her innate sexiness and the fact they were alone and he'd lost sight of reality here. The night had been the stuff of dreams. The way she touched him, the unbelievable sensuousness in everything she did. Part of him wanted to get back over there and kiss her awake *right now*, just pick up where they'd left off, the temptation to throw caution aside almost impossible to resist. He dragged his eyes away from the impossibly long eyelashes lying against her peaches-and-cream complexion and forced himself to think rationally.

The most important thing to him right now was the launch of his kids' courses. He couldn't let himself be distracted from that goal, not by anyone. He'd been working towards it for too long. He'd had his chance to put his own choices first and as a result he'd almost lost Helen. He had no right to pursue his own happiness now, not after the damage that he had done. And if he faced facts, he'd be doing Evie a favour. Better to back off quickly now, clean and sharp, than carry on with this and risk letting her down horribly later. Because that conclusion felt inevitable. It felt *innate*. He wasn't sure he had it in him to be any other way.

Decision made, he stood up and headed for the stream to collect some water. Looking at her sleeping with last night resonating in his mind really didn't lend itself to keeping him focused.

Evie's slowly surfacing sleep-fuzzed brain gradually rolled out questions.

Why so cold?

Why so damned *uncomfortable*? Her shoulder and hip bones ached horribly.

Why so alone?

As that last question crossed her mind, bringing with it all recollection of the night before, her eyes snapped open. A few feet away the fire had burned low. A metal pot perched above it with steam drifting lazily from it.

Mist clung softly to the forest floor. The morning light that filtered through the tree canopy contained not a shred of sunshine. Everything smelled intensely green and damp and her face and shoulders, outside the sleeping bag, were cold. She watched a beetle scurry past her face and climb the nearest plant. She sat up and stretched her aching limbs.

She'd gone to sleep cocooned by Jack, her back against his chest, his arms curled tightly around her, one hand cupping her breast softly beneath her thermal top, his breath warming her neck. Completely exhausted after what felt like hours of greedy indulgence in each other. She'd had no idea making love could be so utterly, deliciously, gorgeously satisfying without *actually* having full-on sex. Not that the desire to go that step further hadn't been tantalisingly present the whole time.

She'd woken up with the sleeping bag to herself.

At some point between then and now, he'd gone. He'd unzipped the sleeping bag and left her to sleep on alone. She glanced around at the snap of a twig from the direction of the stream and he came into view. Fully dressed again in outdoor gear minus the thick padded jacket. He looked utterly gorgeous and her stupid heart gave a twist. She didn't need a confiscated mirror to know she looked and smelled like crap right now. And she wondered why he hadn't hung around in the sleeping bag any longer than he had to.

'Morning,' he said.

'Hi.'

She waited to see what he would follow that up with. Her heartbeat clattered. He nodded towards the fire.

'There's food in that pot for you. Oats cooked with a

little water. We need to get kitted up and ready before the camera crew turn up.'

His voice was matter-of-fact. So no reference to the night before. Just a polite greeting and a tin pot with some kind of hideous pale brown gruel clinging to the bottom. Her heart plummeted lazily in her chest like a punctured balloon. The inevitability of it all made it somehow worse. What had she expected? To wake up in his arms? A morning kiss? Maybe not, but she'd hoped for a bit more than this déjà vu sensation of behaving as if nothing had happened. The soft butterflies in her stomach seemed to have taken on a lurching quality, as if their wings had been clipped.

Give him a chance, Evie.

'What about you?' she said, leaning forward in her sleeping bag and grabbing for a spoon. She pushed the porridge around dubiously. It had the consistency of brown wallpaper paste. 'Aren't you hungry?'

'I've eaten my share,' he said. He was busy picking up camping equipment and packing it into his bag.

'Why didn't you wake me?' she said. 'We could have eaten together.'

He put the bag down and looked at her, his expression giving nothing away.

'It's not exactly croissants and preserves on the veranda,' he said. His tone of voice took on an edge of posh and she felt heat creep up her neck. She'd hoped that the critical spoilt-little-rich-girl references might have been left behind them now.

'I'm always up early, force of habit,' he carried on. 'There's a lot to get through today and I'm not sure the weather's going to be on our side.' He glanced up at the rustling branches high above them as if he expected a hurricane to kick in at any moment. Still no mention of the previous night's activities. He'd reverted to Jack Trent, course leader, expert on the great outdoors predicting the weather. Whatever last night had meant, for him it didn't appear to extend beyond the hours of darkness. A sharp spike of miserable anger kicked into her stomach—anger at herself because she'd dared to hope for more. When had any man she'd been with ever delivered more? How could she have been so stupid as to read anything into last night beyond sex? All those photos she'd seen of him on the Internet with this woman or that woman on his arm. He obviously didn't do meaningful relationships and even if he did, was his first choice ever going to be the girl who'd bad-mouthed him to the country at large?

Her stomach lurched. He was no different from the others after all. Those heady first few dates, feeling as if she'd struck gold. Follow-up phone calls. Texts. Gifts. All so perfect until they got what they wanted, got her into bed and then their interest melted away. She'd fallen for it again and again, the endless hope that this time it would be different. And this one really took the crown.

She ached to put as much distance between herself and Jack Trent as she could, to hole up in her flat and lick her wounds. Instead, she had to stay and see out his horrible TV show, pretending nothing had happened between them, because the only thing worse than being the latest notch on Jack Trent's tent flap would be for the public to find out about it. She could imagine the tabloid glee right now and it made her feel sick.

She stared at the dying fire and collected up her wits, which had been annoyingly absent last night when it had really counted.

There was only one option. Fortunately it was one she'd honed to perfection over the years and all that practice should stand her in good stead now. Gritting her teeth, she took the pot from the fire and channelled I-don't-care for all she was worth. If she was going to be ditched after one night, she would damn well get in first.

'About last night,' she said, not looking at him. Instead she scraped a spoon around the tin of awful porridge. 'It was a mistake.'

CHAPTER NINE

FROM THE CORNER of her eye she saw him stop what he was doing. He turned to face her.

'What?'

She shrugged defiantly.

'Come on. We're both thinking it.'

He raised an eyebrow.

'Are we?'

'Clearly we are,' she said, forcing down a tiny spoonful of the oats. Revolting stodge. Her stomach gave a lazy roll. 'It was a long day yesterday. Last night would never have happened if I'd been thinking straight. And you were up and about the second you woke up and all you've talked about is the outward-bound plan for day two. What other conclusion am I meant to make?'

A distant rumble cut through his silence. It was clear now that a storm was brewing above them. The sky had turned from misty grey to scurrying black in the space of about ten minutes and the tree canopy above them was beginning to whip around. She could feel impending rainfall in the heavy thickness of the air.

He left his bag and crossed to the fire.

'Maybe it would be for the best,' he said, not looking at her.

Oh, what a surprise! There it was right there. One

sentence that proved her right. She tipped her head back and laughed sarcastically up at the angry sky.

'What?' he said.

He stared at her as if he thought she might have gone mad. Maybe she had. Maybe this was what madness was, the same raising of hopes followed by a downward crash, over and over again. She was out of the double sleeping bag in one swift movement, kicking it away, grabbing for her clothes and putting them on. Fast jerky movements that channelled her anger.

'Did I just save you a job?' she asked him. She glanced up at him from lacing up her boots. She shook her head. 'I never learn, do I?' She winked darkly at his confused expression. 'Don't worry, Jack. No need to come up with any lame excuses now, I've saved you the trouble.' She picked up her backpack and began stuffing a few items into it. 'I've probably heard them all before anyway.'

The sky finally burst and fat raindrops began to fall. The tree canopy above them provided some protection, but with the wind whipping the branches about the rainfall made its way through to camp. Light at first, then heavier. The remnants of the fire disappeared with a hiss. Evie did nothing to try and shelter, instead just letting the rain soak and darken her blonde hair. What the hell did a bit of rain matter in the bigger scheme of things? She really couldn't give a damn. Jack stood his ground.

'I should never have let this happen,' he said.

'You did though, didn't you?' she said. 'Didn't have any issues with it last night. Got what you wanted now, no need to keep up any pretence.'

'I'm sorry,' he said. 'It really wasn't like that.'

She stopped packing at the sound of his quiet tone and looked up at him, waiting to see exactly what he might back up an apology with.

'It's not because of anything you've done. I'm not a good person to get involved with, Evie. You're better off without me.'

She stood up angrily.

'Oh, just spare me!' She threw exasperated hands up. 'I thought you might have done a bit better than it's-not-you-it's-me. Have you any idea how many times I've heard that one? You could at least be original.' She leaned down to zip up her backpack. 'You know what? I don't even care. I don't know why I thought you'd be any different. They never are. No one's ever straight with me. You're just like all the others.' She picked up the backpack and hefted it onto her shoulders. He was looking at her in amazement, mouth open. 'Trust me, Jack, because it's tried and tested. It's not bloody you. It actually *is* me.'

She stood facing him tensely across the dead fire, the perfect standoff, and the cameraman trudged into the clearing. He was fresh as a daisy, clean shaven, with a new set of clothes. He looked from one of them to the other.

'Hold that pose, hold that pose,' he gabbled, tugging the handheld camera into position and prising the lens cap off. 'Rough night, was it? Argument? How about an action replay for the viewing public?'

'Oh, piss off!' Evie snapped.

He grinned broadly.

'I see we got out of the wrong side of the sleeping bag this morning,' he said.

Hell, it was like walking across a minefield.

Walking alongside her meant deliberate slowing down of Jack's natural pace but he did it anyway, because she was making no effort whatsoever to walk next to him. Head down, hands thrust into the pockets of her jacket, not speaking. A short hike through the forest brought them out into the open; an hour or so further and they'd be at the site for the planned filming of a list of bush-craft tasks. A few other bits of filming were planned, filler mainly, plus an exit interview with Evie. Who knew how the hell *that* might turn out now? He glanced uneasily up at the sky. Dark clouds scurried across it, blocking out the light. The rain showed no sign of abating.

Guilt churned in his stomach at what she'd said back at the camp, how he'd made her feel. He'd expected anger and blame, had been ready to take full responsibility. He hadn't expected her determination to make his backing off into some failing of hers. He should have seen that coming. She'd spent her whole life feeling not good enough, and now he'd gone and added more fuel to that fire. He'd been too busy thinking about his own inadequacies to think that someone as lovely as her could possibly have some crippling ones of her own.

And he really shouldn't be this concerned about her. When in any of his past liaisons had he given a second thought to how his backing out might make them feel? As far as he was concerned being upfront was enough. He'd never cared enough about them to wonder what the aftermath might be. And he found he couldn't now let this lie. Not like this.

'I meant what I said back at camp,' he said, when the cameraman was out of earshot. He had no idea what he was going to say next.

As she glanced his way he caught sight of an incredulous expression on her face, obviously amazed that he'd opened the subject back up again when she'd already put her own stamp on the situation.

'Forget it,' she said, flapping a dismissive hand at

him. 'I'm not interested. I've been there, done that, and if I had a T-shirt for the number of times a guy's lost interest after the first five minutes, it wouldn't be a jewellery shop I could open. This is no big first for me. So if you don't mind, let's skip the bit where I tell you it doesn't matter so that you can feel better about yourself. I just want this whole thing to be over with.'

She hefted her backpack up higher on her shoulders.

'Let's just get the hell on with the tasks.'

'It has nothing to do with losing interest,' he said, exasperated. 'You think last night was something I do all the time?'

She looked sideways at him, eyebrows slightly raised in challenge.

'I can tell you, it isn't,' he said, holding her gaze until she looked away, almost annoyed at her lack of interest in an explanation. Had last night not even been worth that for her? He glanced behind them to check the cameraman was out of earshot and kept his voice low. 'The press might make it look that way but at least half of those dates *are* actually just dates, believe it or not. No sex involved.'

That got her attention. Rain soaked her hair and clung to her eyelashes and she swiped a hand over her wet cheeks and waited for him to carry on.

'I don't do relationships for a reason, Evie. I've let people down in the past with my behaviour. People who are close to me, people I care about. All because I put myself first.'

'What are you talking about?'

Now would be the moment where he opened up and told her all about Helen. About the way he'd just disappeared into the army without so much as a glance over his shoulder. About coming home to find her hospitalised, broken, weak and his mother desolate that she'd been unable to do anything to stop it. She'd tried for over a week to get hold of him with the news. The familiar dark shame climbed through him, worming its way through his veins as he groped for a way to explain it all that wouldn't bring forth her utter contempt.

She shook her head slowly into the rain-drenched silence.

'I don't want to know. Stick to the plan, Jack. What happened in the Highlands stays in the Highlands. Let's just quit while we're ahead and forget it ever happened.'

The hard stuff had been done on day one, so why the hell didn't it feel like that? No full-on activities today, no cave diving to worry about, no leaping off cliffs. Just a hike back to Jack's activity-centre base of a couple of hours with a few stops thrown in for him to demonstrate navigation skills and emergency measures should you happen to have the appalling luck not only to be caught out in the great outdoors but to be injured too. Each time she'd dutifully stood to one side of the shot and pasted an interested I'm-learning-so-much expression on her face. The minutes dragged by and then she was pulled in to give her opinion on the experience.

What to say...?

She kept her eyes on Jack the entire time as he shifted from foot to foot, clearly sweating after the night and morning they'd just spent together what she might give away on camera. But really, was there ever any question about what she would say?

'So, Evie, how have you found the survival experience as a whole?' Jack asked her, on cue, his voice artificially jovial. He was obviously as anxious to get this over as she was.

She wiped droplets of rain from her face with the back of her hand, gave the viewers what she hoped was a contrite smile and gave them what they wanted. Best for him, best for her. What would be the point in doing anything else? Hadn't the whole point of going through with this weekend been to kill the questioning of Jack Trent's integrity stone dead?

'Tough,' she said. 'But fun.' She held his eyes deliberately. 'The comments I made about your skills that led to this show…well, let's just say I've been proved wrong. In the toughest possible way.' The camera crew provided background chuckles. 'I can honestly say this is an experience I won't forget in a hurry, and I think kids across the country will think Jack's new children's courses are fantastic.'

The camera quit rolling and she followed along with the rest of the team for the final walk back to the centre. All she wanted now was to get back to civilisation with her pride intact and put as much distance between her and Jack Trent as she could. Would she be watching the show when it aired? No. Bloody. Way.

Who needed a massive sunken bath with gold taps?

The no-frills hotel didn't seem half as bad as it had on the way in. Just having an actual *bath* was enough. There was mud in her hair and underneath her fingernails. The girly pink nail varnish she'd had applied back in London just last week was chipped in places, flaking in others. Two of her nails had broken out in the field and in the absence of anything so civilised as nail scissors she'd gnawed them to get rid of any sharp edges. She removed the remaining traces of varnish while the bath filled, tipping the entire contents of the one-product-fits-all bath/shower/shampoo combo under the running water. A fresh unisex citrus scent filled the steamy room and she couldn't have revelled in it more if it were a top-of-the-range designer scent.

Her hair felt gritty at the roots. She let herself sink slowly down beneath the surface of the warm water, closed her eyes and tried not to think about Jack Trent.

For a moment back there it had felt different. Real. He'd seen her at her absolute worst and liked her, *preferred* her in fact to when she was playing her best. To Evie that was the stuff of dreams and somehow that made it worse. He'd looked beyond the TV personality that her previous boyfriends had been interested in; she'd trusted him enough to show him that. He'd seen the real Evie, and she'd fallen short. By morning they might have still been in the forest but he'd behaved just like every other guy she'd dated, looking for a handy get-out.

That wasn't strictly true.

Easy to lump his rejection in with all the others. The fact remained that he'd tried to give her some kind of explanation, not that she'd given him the chance. What might he have said if she'd let him carry on with that explanation instead of cutting him off?

She sat up in the bath and quickly washed her hair using the shower attachment, all the while focusing hard on the positives. Raking over this stuff was completely futile. Whatever had been between her and Jack Trent was done with, and picking through it in her mind was pointless. She came out of this situation with a new contract right when she needed it and a knock-on boost to her jewellery brand. She should be delighted.

If only that success didn't feel now as if it came with strings. As if it were diminished. Could her jewellery hold its own without the Miss K name to buoy it up? She'd been too scared to find out, had jumped at the chance of the TV tie-in for her designs instead of standing or falling on her own merit alone. But now the fact she hadn't tried and would never know needled at her in a way it hadn't before.

The knock on the door came as she combed out her wet hair, bringing a sense of déjà vu that made her pulse jump. A couple of days ago and she'd opened the door to find Jack leaning on one huge shoulder against the door frame.

This time it really *was* just a room service lasagne.

No frills, but she really couldn't give a toss. She tucked in anyway, savouring every mouthful and stuffing the whole thing including the hunk of garlic bread on the side. It was the best lasagne she'd ever tasted.

Afterwards she opened the door, wearing the sleep shorts and vest she'd brought along with her. This hotel was not the kind that laid on fluffy white bathrobes or complimentary chocolates. She knelt down and put the tray of empty crockery on the floor to one side of the door, as requested in the laminated room service instructions.

A pair of trainers came to a standstill next to the tray and she looked up from her hands and knees, past the jeans and tight-fitting grey T-shirt.

'I don't want it to just stay in the Highlands,' Jack said.

Evie's wide blue eyes stayed on his as she got to her feet. The vest-and-shorts combo she was wearing revealed smooth bath-pink skin and her hair lay in damp tendrils against her bare neck. She was utterly gorgeous and his head spun with latent desire for her. Reservations were left behind as he followed his instincts. In one swift movement she was in his arms. He slid his hands around her slender waist and groped for her mouth with his, found it and kissed and kissed and kissed her. As he picked her up she hooked her long legs around his back as he blindly walked her back into her hotel room. Her dinner tray clattered as he accidentally kicked it on the way past. Heedless of the cutlery flying across the hallway, he kicked the door shut behind them with his foot.

There were no cumbersome clothes to manoeuvre around this time. Steam hung in the air from the tiny en-suite bathroom. Through its open door he could see the steamed-up mirror and the pile of dark outdoor clothes on the bathroom floor where she'd left them. She smelled and tasted squeaky clean, like lemons, and he let himself sink deliciously into unconsciousness of everything except the way she tasted and smelled and felt beneath his hands. He took her in with all five senses, and everything about her was perfect.

Evie buried her face in his neck, breathing in the scent of his warm skin. Even scrubbed up, he smelled of the great outdoors. His aftershave had fresh woody notes, like the forest after rain.

He carried her to the bed as if she weighed nothing, not letting up for a second with his kisses. They were deep and hungry, as if he couldn't get enough of her, and that sensation alone sent hot thrills curling through her. The feeling was inherent in his every touch of her that he was savouring this, that this wasn't some quick throwaway screw. His tongue slipped softly against hers, his fingers tangled gently in her hair.

As he reached the end of the single bed he eased her slowly backwards, a dizzying sensation of softly falling, until her head was on the pillow and he was looming above her.

His hands found the hem of her vest and pushed it

softly up and over her head to be cast randomly away in some corner of the room. Exposed, her bath-warm nipples scrunched in surprise at the sudden cool air and he took advantage, trailing kisses down from her neck and past the hollow between her collarbones to close his lips over the hard peaks. He sucked them gently in turn as she sighed and arched her back.

As he trailed a line of kisses down the hollow of her stomach her mind followed every movement of his lips while her breath shortened and her pulse jumped. Her loose sleep shorts were gone in one gentle tug and then his breath was warm at the tingling core of her as he parted her softly with his tongue. Gentle fingertips caressed her inner thighs and moved lower to lightly tease her entrance while he made lingering delicate strokes with his tongue at the most sensitive nub. Soon she was a writhing mass of desire on the bed, aching for him to go further, wanting him inside her. He played on that need until the wait was too much and she grabbed a rough handful of his T-shirt and tugged until he relented and stood up.

The gorgeous eyes held hers as he reached behind his head and removed his T-shirt while her breath came in short bursts. He removed his jeans and as he cast them to one side he pulled a foil packet from one of the pockets. He'd come here wanting this, then. Wanting *her*. He knew her without all the trappings that she'd relied on for so long to make her appealing and desirable. She was enough to hold his interest after all, the real Evie, trapped underneath all those years of trying to fit in, of trying to be everything to everyone, of vying for attention in any way she could.

As he slid smoothly inside her she raised her lips to meet his. His thrusts were slow and deep, building a delicious friction that took her higher and higher until she was curling her legs around him, raking her nails across the rock-hard muscles of his back, moving with him to find that perfect dizzying height of pleasure.

CHAPTER TEN

THE EVENING CREPT towards night. She lay now in the crook of his arm, curled up tightly against him in the narrow single bed. Hours later and he was still there.

He'd thought this afternoon, making his way to her room almost on autopilot, that maybe it could just be about the sex. Because for all the deliciousness of their sleeping-bag encounter in the forest, there had been a sense of incompleteness about it. A night spent exploring each other in the firelight, an experience so in tune with his own most base pleasures—the fresh outdoor air on their skin, the green scent and night sounds of the forest filling his senses. The maddening desire to screw her, to go to that ultimate level, had been foiled at the time.

He'd wondered if this crazed inability to just let her go was down to that: a need for physical closure. Yet now he had that, her warm breath against his chest, her sleeping fingers entwined in his, and it wasn't enough. He'd believed he could walk away and he was wrong. There was no place in the universe right now that he would rather be.

The glow from the basic table lamp was soft as he took a lock of her hair between his fingers, twirling it, marvelling at how perfectly she seemed to fit in his arms. Lying with someone wasn't usually part of the remit. For a while after leaving the army, free of its constraints, he'd had a run of very short-term relationships, generally with women he picked up casually, easy flings to walk away from. Staying the night had never been a big thing for him; he liked his privacy too much. The longer you spent with someone, the more questions they asked, the more of your life you were expected to share. He hadn't wanted that so he'd kept his distance.

'I didn't think I'd see you again,' she said, her breath warm against his chest. 'Except possibly for on TV.'

He glanced down at the top of her golden head.

'Thanks,' he said.

'What for?'

'The round-up of the show that you did. For getting in the mention of the kids' courses. You didn't have to do that.'

Her voice was neutral.

'You're welcome. I thought it would make us even. Get through the show, clear your name, get my life back.'

'The way I behaved back in the forest... I wanted to make you understand and I made a crap job of it. I couldn't get a word in—you had the whole thing straight in your own mind, but I shouldn't have let that stop me.'

She propped herself up on one elbow and looked at him.

'I don't have a great track record when it comes to men,' she said. 'Half the people they talk about in the press are just guys who happened to be at the same party as me, or who I've spoken to for five minutes. Then I open the newspaper the following morning and I'm meant to be having a relationship with them.' She rested her chin on her hand, lying against his chest. 'I never bothered contradicting any of it. Chester has this mantra that any publicity—'

'Is good publicity,' he said. 'Yeah, I got that.'

Was there nothing her insane agent wouldn't do?

'The few that I actually *have* dated never amounted to much,' she said, her face thoughtful. 'It all starts out peachy and I'll be lulled into thinking it might actually be the real deal for once, and then it turns out all they really want to do is party. They want to be seen out on the town. Then they might ask about being on the TV show. Or doing a joint photo shoot maybe.' She put on a sarcastic voice. 'That kind of thing. When they realise I'm not the party animal they thought I was, they lose interest.'

She kissed his chest lightly, sending a new wave of heat through his body.

'The TV-image thing isn't something I blab about to just anyone. I'd never met anyone like you before. You had no time for me at all when I was channelling full-on TV-show diva—you were far more interested when I was smothered in mud and stinky.'

He grinned.

'You were never stinky.'

She smiled.

'I really liked that so much about you, that you seemed interested in what I'm really like instead of the TV image. I used to put on an act when I was growing up too. I was sent to boarding school not long after my mother died, and it was really hard. Pretending to be someone else was the only thing that helped. I hid all my homesickness behind this crazy girl who would do anything for a laugh. For the first time in my life I was suddenly cool. I had loads of friends. I was the centre of attention.'

She looked across the room at the darkened window.

Outside the wind was still blustering, whipping across the hotel car park, pattering the glass with rain.

'Not sure I liked that crazy schoolgirl much myself though. Who would have thought that at twenty-five I'd still have an alter ego? Not so much crazy school-girl any more, though. More rich princess now.' She shifted uncomfortably. 'Not sure I like her much either.' She sighed. 'When you backtracked the morning after I just assumed you were like everyone else, saying what I wanted to hear at first and then backing off the moment you had time to think it through. Intrigued by me until the novelty was out of the way.'

He found her hand and wrapped his fingers around hers.

'It had nothing to do with your TV image at all,' he said. 'Everything you said about your TV stuff made perfect sense. The way you acted up when you were on camera, how different you were when you were on your own with me.' He paused while he dredged up the words from the depths of him. 'It had more to do with the fact that I don't make a habit of getting to know people. I don't talk about my private life,' he said.

'I know,' she said. 'I spent ages doing a detailed web and social-media search on you. You never talk about anything outside your charity stuff and your survival skills.'

'That's deliberate.'

'Why? You have something to hide?'

She said it in a half jokey tone but he didn't smile back and the light-hearted expression faded from her face.

'What is it?'

She sat up, the sheet held across her chest.

He shrugged, looking up at her from the pillow.

'In the car you talked about school, about how you acted up so you could fit in.'

She nodded.

'I could relate to that,' he said.

She raised her eyebrows.

'Really?'

'Not the posh school,' he said, rolling his eyes. 'I mean peer pressure. That need to be accepted, to fit in, no matter what it takes. My school was this hideous inner-city place, rough as hell. I didn't want to be there any more than half the other kids did. I bunked off school more than I was there. The thing is, you take that structure out of a teenager's life, take away any authority figures, throw in a group of mates all in the same situation. What you get is a melting pot of boredom. None of us had any money. It was all my mother could do to put food on the table.'

The usual gag of shame rose in his mouth at the thought of his mother, working three horrible jobs to keep a horrible roof over him and Helen while he was out all hours just hanging around with his horrible mates.

'It must have been tough,' Evie said.

He looked up at the ceiling, decorative swirls in the peeling plaster. She curled her hand into his and he liked it.

'I ended up getting mixed up in some bad stuff.'

'Stuff?'

He took a breath.

'Vandalism. Stealing cars. Stuff that was a springboard to more trouble.'

She didn't move, although he'd half expected her to stand up and head for the bathroom. To get in a bit of distance.

'It was just a matter of time before I got hauled in

by the police. Then one day we torched a car and the police picked up a couple of my mates. I was this close to being taken in too except that they only had circumstantial evidence.' He held up his thumb and forefinger with a tiny gap between them. 'The police came to the flat and horrified my mother. And then my grandfather stepped in. Gave me a real talking-to about turning my life around, told me I was responsible for my mother and sister.'

'And what did you do? Did you get yourself sorted out?'

'Yeah, I got myself sorted, all right,' he said. He could hear the contempt for himself lacing his own voice. 'No doubt about that. I'm not sure it was exactly what my grandfather meant though.'

'How do you mean?'

She was staring at him, sharply interested.

He shrugged.

'I joined up. I got the hell out of there. And I did turn my life around.'

She was nodding.

'I read about your military record. It was impressive.'

He shook his head at her, dismissing that. Any pride that he might have had in his military performance was tainted.

'It was the responsibility for my mother and sister part that I screwed up,' he said.

'How do you mean?'

He chanced a glance her way. Her blue eyes were screwed up in a frown.

'My grandfather meant keeping my nose clean, finding a job, taking some of the burden away from my mother. I should have stayed in London, turned my life around and been there for my family. But I knew I wasn't strong enough to avoid the guys I hung around with and so I took the selfish option.'

'In what universe is joining the army the selfish option?' she said, holding up a hand.

'You don't get it,' he said. 'It was all about starting a new life instead of fixing the old one. *For me.* I left my mum and Helen behind in the same place. Same poverty trap. Same three jobs for my mother, same awful prospects for Helen. And the worst of it was that I didn't give either of them a second thought. Finding the army was a revelation, all the things I'd been missing. Training, structure, hierarchy, consequences. And I loved the physical side of it. It was exactly what my life lacked.'

'I don't understand why you feel bad about that,' she said. 'Surely your family must have been so proud of you, taking control of your life like that, pulling things around. I know how I feel about Will. The army is everything to him—it's what he was born to do. I'm sure your sister must feel the same about you.'

'It's not the same for your brother,' he said. Of course she saw it that way because she had her own military family background to reference things by. Her brother would have gone straight in as an officer from Sandhurst after public school. It was a whole different world from Jack's experience. 'Leaving you to join up meant leaving you with your own secure flat and a trust fund to look after you. I left Helen behind with nothing. Gradually I stopped hearing from them. Letters tailed off. Phone calls got skipped. It didn't even register at first, I was so preoccupied with my work. I only realised how bad things were when my mother finally got word to me that Helen was in hospital. She'd overdosed.'

'A suicide attempt? Oh, Jack.'

He shook his head. That had been his own horrified first reaction too, when he'd heard.

'A drug overdose,' he said. 'Not intentional. She was an addict. Her dealer was one of my so-called mates and I wasn't there to stop it.'

She frowned as if she was making sense of it all.

'That's why your charity work is all for youth drug organisations,' she said.

He nodded.

'I wasn't there when Helen needed me. As soon as I realised how bad things were I left the forces, came home and looked for a new direction. I got Helen into rehab, found somewhere new for them to live. All things I should have done months if not years earlier, except that I was too busy doing what *I* wanted. The kids' courses came a long time later. By then I had the TV interest in my survival stuff. I thought the courses might be an alternative for vulnerable kids to spend their time instead of hanging around street corners, getting into trouble.'

He forced himself to hold her gaze.

'I'm crap relationship material, Evie. I let down the most important person in my life because I was selfish. My work is my way of making up for that. I can't let myself be distracted from that. You deserve to be with someone who will always put you first and that's not been my strong point.'

She wasn't walking away. Had she not heard what he said? Instead she leaned in slowly and kissed him on the mouth. His heart turned over in his chest at the gentleness of it.

'You're not responsible for Helen's drug addiction,' she said quietly. 'You weren't even there. So you made a mistake in the past. We've all done that, Jack. Just look at me with my foot in my mouth. You can't control how other people behave, and you've done all you can to put things right. Who's to say she wouldn't have had the same problems even if you'd been living at home?'

'She wouldn't,' he said shortly. 'I would have looked out for her.'

Evie could tell just from the stubborn subject-closed tone of his voice that he wasn't about to be convinced otherwise. Sympathy for him flooded through her, along with a happy little flash that this, with him, this really was different after all. He'd been trying, in some crazy way, to protect her by backing away. Her mind processed all that he'd told her and in a flash of clarity she realised why he didn't give interviews, why the publicity around him only vaguely touched on his past.

'All this is why you're so cagey about your private life,' she said.

He nodded.

'I don't want Helen's problems dredged up.'

His sense of responsibility for his sister touched Evie deeply. Who did she have in her life that felt that way about her? She couldn't help being drawn to that side of him.

'The last thing Helen needs is for all this to be made public. She's got her life back on track. She's going to college now. So I keep my private life well away from the TV stuff.'

'Do I count as TV stuff?' she said then.

'You're kind of becoming a bit of a grey area.' She was relieved to see a smile touch his lips. 'I kind of thought you'd be running for the hills.'

She smiled at him.

'I'm not going anywhere. Not until tomorrow. I'm flying from Inverness. I'll be out of your hair before you know it.'

'I quite like you in my hair,' he said softly.

CHAPTER ELEVEN

THREE WEEKS NOW since the weekend in the Highlands, during which the TV show had aired to a fantastic reception. Any residual fear that Jack's interest in her would diminish in direct proportion to their growing time apart had turned out to be unfounded. His work commitments had rocketed since the roll-out of the first kids' courses, but still he texted when he said he would, he phoned when he said he would. He was always on time when he visited. In that he really did remind her of the men in her family—that military organisation that became so ingrained that it was a part of their personality.

In Jack she found she liked it. She found herself relying on him now because she knew she could.

There was just the secrecy thing.

She'd agreed with him right away that it was best to keep a low profile for now. How could she disagree after what he'd confided in her about Helen? The media interest in the joint show had led to scrutiny of them both and he refused to do anything that might drag his sister and her problems into the limelight.

But now the show had aired and his desire to keep their—*relationship*?—whatever this was under wraps showed no sign of declining. While his explanation for it made perfect sense there was still a prickling insecurity deep inside her that his reluctance to shout it from the rooftops had more to do with her than it did Helen. His sister's overdose was a few years ago. She was settled now, as was his mother, the newsworthiness of their past surely diminished through the passage of time. The thought nagged at her, deep inside. Was it instead just a handy excuse to stop things between them getting too full-on?

Now he'd spent a third night in as many weeks at her Chelsea flat. They'd had food delivered rather than go out, making the most of each other's company. Jack had never felt so settled. The ability to offload without judgement, to share his work plans with someone instead of working all hours and going home to his own company, was great. The sense of isolation brought on by keeping everything to himself had been so acute that he hadn't realised how alone he was until now. She made him talk things over. She was interested in him.

Things were good.

The phone rang in the hallway and she padded out across the bare wood floor to pick up.

Her shoulders sagged visibly and he watched from the kitchen as she turned away from him, one hand creeping upwards to sink itself into her hair. She walked away from him. Far enough to be out of listening range, not that he needed to hear what was being said to see that she was uncomfortable. Her answers were short. The entire conversation lasted only a minute or two and then she put the phone down on the table and crossed the room back to him, her eyes clouded, gnawing at her thumbnail.

'Who was that?'

She shook her head lightly and offered him a smile. 'My father.'

He followed her into the sitting room. She sat down on the oatmeal sofa, her expression thoughtful.

'Don't tell me,' he joked, holding up a hand. 'You want to introduce me.'

'He called to tell me he'll be staying in the house in France for the next three weeks,' she said as if he hadn't spoken. 'A "nice escape from the tabloid media", he called it. Had to get *that* dig in, of course. He wanted to make sure I knew he was there in case I tip up unexpectedly and we're forced to do anything so off the wall as actually spend time in the same house together.'

She spoke with pure sarcasm but he knew her well enough by now to pick up on the tics. The way she folded her arms across her body, that tight expression on her face that gave nothing away. He moved to sit next to her, put his arm around her and tugged her against him. The dark pink sofa cushions were sinkably soft. A huge flatscreen TV hung on the opposite wall. She hadn't been joking about liking a box set, and so far she'd seemed happy to stay at home with him, cooking or having takeout. Party girl really had been a persona she put on when she left the flat.

'Ah, well, meeting your girlfriend's father isn't something you rush to do as a bloke,' he said. 'There's this kind of unspoken power-struggle thing with girlfriends' fathers. You know, no one is ever good enough for their little girl and all that.'

She shook her head, a wry smile touching her lips.

'You're mistaking my father for someone who gives a toss.' She leaned back on the sofa and looked at him. 'He'd like you. You've got that military thing going on that all the men in my family have. And he likes your show.' She shrugged. 'Although you've probably ruined that by having me on it.'

'Has it always been this tense between you?' he asked carefully. 'I remember you mentioned he wasn't around much when you were at school.'

'He was around when I got into trouble,' she said.

'What about when you were a kid though, the camping holidays you told me about?'

'That was different. My mum was around back then.' She leaned back on the sofa and looked up at the ceiling. 'It's like you could draw a line in the sand. Split up everything before and after that point.'

He thought briefly of his own mother, bringing him and Helen up by herself, doing whatever it took to keep things going.

'What was she like?'

She thought it over.

'She was hands-on in a way my father's never managed to be. She had Will and me going to the village school, mixing with local kids, playing outdoors. Family holidays. My father's army leave was packed with day trips she'd organised, fun things to do.' She smiled at him briefly and then looked down at her hands. 'She was killed in a car accident. All very sudden and unexpected. Immediately my father slid the whole lot of us into stiff-upper-lip army mode. Our lives were reorganised, new schools, nannies. Grieving never really made it into the process. Perhaps he thought it might make Will and me feel secure, but the change was so radical we were both gobsmacked by it. It took me years to feel even remotely settled anywhere.'

'Maybe that was the only way he knew of dealing with it,' Jack said. 'Not that I'm making excuses for him, but when you've been in the army organisation and discipline can become so ingrained that it's hard to do anything on an emotional level. It's all about order. Maybe it was his way of keeping control.'

She seemed to ponder that for a moment.

'There was more to it than that,' she said. 'It's complicated.'

'In what way?'

She looked at him carefully as if she was debating what to say.

'When I was fourteen he came to my school to sort out some scrape or other I'd got into,' she said. 'I'd had to act up for him to even acknowledge I was alive. I wonder sometimes if I hadn't made him so angry whether he'd ever have told me.'

'Told you what?' She wasn't making any sense.

She swallowed hard enough for him to hear the click in her throat.

'He isn't my real father,' she said.

He stared at her.

It was the first time she'd said it out loud. Now it was out there it was as if she couldn't stop. She ran a distracted hand through her hair.

'I'm not a real Staverton-Lynch. I don't know masses of details. He didn't tell me much and I've no one else I can ask. My mother and father were childhood friends, in touch throughout school and university. At some point my mother drifted into a bad relationship and when she found she was pregnant the guy just left her. My father was there for her. He supported her through it.' She glanced up at him. 'And he claimed the baby—me—as his own.'

His face was a picture.

'This is unbelievable,' he said.

'I know. You should try being part of it,' she said.

'And he treated you as his child?'

She nodded.

'While my mum was alive, yes. But after she died it became clear that he did that for her sake, not because he really thought of me like that. Looking back, I knew something was different from the moment she'd gone. He was different with me straight away, withdrawn, distant.' She let her mind drift back down the years. The memory made her throat constrict and she bit her lip hard. 'I just couldn't fathom what had changed. I spent years trying to get his attention. Any attention would have done, just for him to look at me again the way he used to.' She shrugged. 'He never did, of course, because his regard for me was completely dependent on my mum being there. He did it for her, not for me. That day at the school he told me he'd continue to support me for my mother's sake. I would remain a Staverton-Lynch and the whole thing would be confidential.' She leaned forward and touched his arm urgently. 'No one knows about this, Jack. You mustn't tell anyone. Even my brother isn't aware of it.'

He let out a long breath.

'What about your real father?'

The familiar hard tightening in her chest as she thought of him.

'He walked away from my mother and me before I was born and he's never been in touch since,' she said. 'Whatever I might think about John Staverton-Lynch, we both loved my mother. We still do. That's the one thing we really have in common. What he does, even now, he does for her, and I don't want to mess with that.' She paused. 'I would like to be loved like that.'

The ache in her voice, ill-hidden, tore at Jack's heart.

'When *Miss Knightsbridge* took off I couldn't believe how nice people were to me all of a sudden. How interested.' She smiled a little. 'That all seems so shallow now, the wanting-public-approval thing, but for a while there I was really carried away by it. I bought into it so much that I ended up being taken in by men who were never really interested in me at all. Not until you, anyway.'

His innate protectiveness kicked in and he slipped an arm around her and tugged her against him. She leaned into his embrace. All that bravado and in-your-face attitude had been a protective barrier between her and the rest of the world, and she'd chosen to let him see past it. He was touched.

'That girl on screen, the one I first met in the production office that day, she's two-dimensional,' he said into her hair. 'Some mad reflection of how you think people want to see you. Why the hell should you care so much what people think about you?'

'I know I shouldn't. My rational mind tells me that. I'm not a complete idiot. But everything that's happened to me tells me otherwise. Oh, I was always well looked after. I still am—I mean, look at this place.' She waved a hand around her to take in the glossy flat. 'But in terms of affection, of being loved or actually even *liked*—that was dependent on my mother being here.'

She leaned forward and put her elbows on her knees, her hands raking back into her blonde hair. He slid from the sofa next to her to kneel on the floor and peel her hands gently from her face.

'You are lovely,' he said. '*You.* Without reference to anyone else, real or imagined, past or present.'

She looked sideways up at him and gave him a half-grin.

'I've never met anyone who cared so much what other people thought of them,' he said. 'And fitting in is a big deal for anyone. Hell, I threw away my teens on exactly that. But don't let it stifle who you really are. You don't need approval from the world or the media or me or anyone else.'

He slid his palms against her cheeks, his fingers raking gently back into her hair, and tipped her face to meet his so he could press the point with his eyes. She covered his hands with her own and moved in to kiss him, wrapping her arms around his neck, pushing him backwards until he was on his back with the soft rug beneath him.

He *got* her. The sensation of relying on someone, of knowing that she had his support, made her feel as if she could conquer the world without any pretence. Being herself was good enough for him. Did he have any idea what that meant to her?

Her every movement was deliberately slow. A tender intimacy that had been altogether missing from any encounters Jack had had with women before.

He realised now that this wasn't anything so easy to categorise as an 'encounter', which meant it was equally impossible to write off as anything similarly throwaway. Not a fling. Not a one-night stand. He didn't want it to end. He was greedy to share not just time with her, not just a bed, but what was going on in her mind, the highs and lows.

The revelation of how in deep he really was took his breath away. There was a sliver of his mind that told him to run for the hills, a voice that had held great clout with him for the longest time. With her he had the ability to tune it out.

As she slowly undressed him and tugged him to the thick rug on the floor, as she knelt deliciously naked astride him, all the time her blue eyes fixed on his, one small hand pressed lightly on his chest. As she ground her hips against him, sometimes circling, sometimes moving up and down in a slow deliberate rhythm, he saw how much she'd come to mean to him and instead of denying himself that pleasure, not just their physical but their emotional connection, he embraced every second of it.

'I'm sorry, I must have heard you wrong.'

There was a loud clatter as Chester let his latte cup fall into its saucer. He leaned forward across the table as customers rubbernecked across the smart café, incredulous eyebrows practically disappearing into his quiff hairstyle.

'For a moment there I thought you suggested *delaying* signing up for a second series of *Miss Knightsbridge*.' He cackled madly. 'Which of course you couldn't have, because that would be *career suicide*.'

Evie took a nervous sip of her own coffee.

'I'm not saying I won't sign, I'm just asking you, as my agent—' she emphasised that last part in the hope that it might remind Chester exactly who was paying whom here '—to negotiate a little bit more time before I do.' She took a calming breath. 'I have a few issues I need to think over first.'

Like exactly whether she could stomach being someone else again for months of filming after the freedom of these last few weeks with Jack. Not to mention the impact that being in the public eye, which had seemed so important to her a month or so ago, would have on this whatever-this-was that was happening between them.

'What the hell is there to think over? You're hardly in a position to negotiate after your libellous comment went public.' He held up a hand as she opened her mouth to butt in. 'OK, so you've smoothed that over with the joint survival show and that's exactly why you sign up *now*, while the offer's on the table, while Purple Productions are still basking in the success of the one-off show. Just what the hell are these few issues that are so damn important?'

She shrugged and toyed with her coffee cup.

'I've been seeing rather a lot of Jack Trent,' she said quietly. She glanced up at Chester. 'We've become quite close since we filmed the TV show.'

Chester's eyes widened and his face broke into an enormous grin as if he'd just unwrapped an amazing present. He held up a hand.

'Stop. Backtrack a moment there. You mean to tell me you and Jack Trent are an item?'

She shrugged.

'Kinda.'

There was a scrape as Chester pushed his chair back and joined her on the sofa opposite. He put an arm around her shoulders and squeezed.

'Why didn't you *say*?'

'Because Jack doesn't do publicity. He's about the nearest thing you can get to a recluse while still appearing on TV. I'm worried that the interest from *Miss Knightsbridge* will drag his private life into the spotlight.'

These last few weeks had been so delicious and she wanted that feeling to stay on. Wanted Jack to know she was prepared to make compromises for the sake of their relationship. And the idea of winding down on some of the crazy *Miss K* publicity was suddenly very appealing to her too. The more time she spent being herself with Jack out of the spotlight, the harder it felt to put on that front.

He held up his hands.

'Enough said. I've navigated my way through the tricky waters of the media for *hundreds* of clients and I can do the same for you and Jack.'

'Really?'

He patted her hand.

'Sweetie, have I ever let you down? You know you can trust me to do whatever's best for your career. Now, let's get another coffee over here and you can tell me *all* about it.'

He snapped his fingers for the waitress's attention.

Evie perched on the orange sofa as a make-up artist dashed on set and dusted her face with a huge powder brush. She tried not to notice that the girl took far longer than was necessary to do the same to Jack, who might have been sitting next to her but was keeping a gap between them that said platonic. His face was a tense mask. The TV show logo—*Hot Breakfast*, in gaudy sunshine-orange letters—was everywhere she looked, and they'd be on air in a matter of minutes.

She spoke in an audible whisper through her beaming teeth.

'You could look a bit more enthusiastic. Chester manages to line up a prime TV interview exclusively about your kids' courses and you look like you're going to the gallows. Think of the publicity.'

Since her chat with Chester he'd certainly stepped up to the plate with his publicity machine, generously lining up some promo for Jack alongside the work he did for her. She was along this morning to give her own take on the course content after the tasks she'd done on the joint TV show.

'I'm not comfortable with this stuff, you know that,' he hissed back.

The interview began with a clip of the highlights of her own *Survival Camp Extreme* experience, laughably referred to as her 'best bits', followed by some footage of gleeful muddy eleven-year-olds taking part in one of Jack's courses.

'...and since the success of the *Survival Camp* TV shows, Jack Trent has recently launched a completely new initiative, run through schools, aimed at nine- to fourteen-year-olds. Looks like they're having great fun there.' The presenter laughed lightly. 'Just give us an idea of the course content, Jack.'

Evie watched him on the monitor as the camera zoomed in for a close-up, talking animatedly now he was talking about his passion. The blonde female presenter leaned in, piling on the praise, twinkling at him. She felt a burst of *he's mine* exasperation. Of course no one knew he was hers, a situation he seemed in no rush to correct.

'And what about you, Evie? What was your take on the skills these courses involve? You got to try them out firsthand.'

The presenter beamed at her. Evie smiled, loving the opportunity to praise Jack up.

'It was a challenge, I can't deny that,' she said. 'But also terrific fun.' How easy it was to fudge the truth. Parts of it had been a living hell. 'We're so used to being surrounded by technology these days...with social media, computer games, TV...that it's great to take away all these trappings for once, learn some physical skills and enjoy the great outdoors. It's hard at first but it's very rewarding and it's been a huge success so far, mainly down to Jack's hard work.'

She smiled sideways at him.

The glossy presenter leaned back.

'It must be great for Jack to have your support. You two seem very close,' she purred at them. 'There's been a lot of rumours to that effect.'

She smiled knowingly as a shot of Jack and Evie sitting shoulder to shoulder after the river crossing was flashed up. He had his arm around her and her head was leaned gently in against him. The body language was all there. A smile touched Evie's lips before she could stop it. The natural response now would be to come clean to the viewing public. The perfect opportunity. They were a couple. The whole world knew it already anyway. She waited for Jack to give a you've-got-me laugh and confirm the rumours. The camera zoomed in for a close-up.

'That picture was taken after a particularly gruelling river crossing,' Jack said gruffly. He sat up straight-backed, his whole demeanour screaming defensive.

She turned her head towards him as if in a dream.

'So there's no truth in the rumours that you two are a couple?' the presenter cajoled, obviously desperate for the scoop on live TV.

'We are absolutely *not* an item,' he snapped. 'We've worked together on one occasion and we share a production company. That's all there is to it. We're friends. I didn't come on here to discuss my personal life.'

'Whoa, OK,' the presenter said, holding her hands up in mock defence. 'Anything to add to that, Evie?'

Jack glanced sideways at her and her stomach gave a miserable lurch. She could feel warmth climbing from the collar of the silk shirt she wore, undoubtedly turning her a shade of red that would clash horribly with the *Hot Breakfast* logo. He'd just denied her to the world.

'We're just friends,' she corroborated dully. Her voice sounded somehow thick, as if she needed to swallow.

It took five minutes more before the interview was wrapped up and she didn't hear a word of it.

She somehow managed to keep her composure until they'd left the TV studios and made it back to her flat. The last thing she needed was a brand-new public scandal. She could just imagine the headline: *Evie Staverton-Lynch in blazing public row with Jack Trent.* Instead she tried her best to channel ice-cold not bothered when her heart felt as if it had been stamped on.

He'd denied her. To the world on live TV. Could there *be* a worse denial than that?

She could understand him not going out of his way to broadcast their relationship. After all, what did she expect him to do, issue a joint statement like some kind of sodding movie star? But this was him being put on the spot. And he'd given an active declaration to the very clear contrary. He didn't need to confirm anything. He could have kept silent, although even that might have looked a bit odd, given the jovial tone of the interview. Instead he'd made it crystal clear that there was nothing going on between them.

There was only one conclusion she could make: he was embarrassed to be dating her. Cold, miserable shame crept through her.

As soon as they were in the hallway of her flat she closed the door on the prying outside world and turned to face him, forcing herself to speak naturally, as if she weren't in agony inside. The bliss of finding him, someone at last who genuinely liked her, who didn't care about any of the Staverton-Lynch rich connotations, who knew about her past and wanted her anyway. It had been the stuff of dreams. The only problem was he didn't feel strongly enough about any of that to actually *tell* anyone.

He'd known right away from her stricken expression back on the TV-show sofa what he'd done. She'd seemed fine with keeping their relationship quiet, never pushing things. Funny how easy it had been to slip into sharing someone else's company. In the short few weeks after the joint-survival TV show had aired they'd grabbed time together whenever they could, but it hadn't amounted to more than a couple of evenings because he'd been wrapped up in the launch of the kids' courses. It suited him. From steadfastly single guarding your private life like a Rottweiler, it was an odd change to find yourself wanting to be with someone, wanting to share your time with them.

They were taking it slowly and he liked that. He *needed* that. Keeping the relationship between the two of them somehow defused the sense of it being serious that made him so uneasy. On some subconscious level, it couldn't be completely real and serious if no one knew about it. And that meant it was safe. No fear of getting close and then letting her down. They couldn't be close when it was this casual—right? She seemed happy to keep things casual, fit them in around their other commitments. So far it was the best thing that had happened to him in years.

And now it turned out that wasn't enough. She'd obviously just been waiting for him to take the relationship to the next level. He wasn't sure he was up to that.

'You know how I feel about keeping out of the limelight,' he said before she could speak, trying to defuse the situation. 'The TV shows are one thing—that doesn't give them the right to my private life.'

She held his gaze steadily, her chin tilted up defiantly. It didn't hide the crushed look in her eyes.

'OK, you like your privacy,' she managed. 'I *get* that.

I know you don't want your past dredged up for whatever reason and that's fine. But I never suggested we do a joint bloody photo shoot, for Pete's sake.' She held her hands up to highlight an imaginary banner headline. '"At home with Evie and Jack as they relax in Evie's Chelsea apartment." I didn't want any of that.'

She lowered her voice.

'I didn't expect you to shout it from the rooftops. I know that isn't you. All I wanted was no denials.'

'It wasn't about denying you. Denying us.'

She shook her head and laughed darkly.

'What the hell was it about, then? Because it sounded an awful lot like a denial to me, Jack. I was there. I'd say it would be hard to be any more categorical.'

'The presenter put me on the spot,' he said. 'I had no idea that question was coming. It was a split-second choice.'

She held up a hand as he groped for an explanation that might actually sound a bit less crap without giving away the fact that as relationships went he was the worst choice on the planet.

'Don't you see? That's exactly the problem,' she said. 'You shouldn't even need to make a split-second choice. The fact you needed to think about it at all is the problem. I wanted you to be happy with me. Proud to be with me.'

Her voice cracked and he took a desperate step towards her, wanting to undo this, seeing that he'd tried to make this work on terms that would keep her safe and had ended up hurting her anyway. She took a compensatory step backwards.

'I am proud to be with you,' he said. It sounded so utterly lame now, when he'd demonstrated exactly the opposite on national television.

She circled him in the hallway, walked the few steps back to the door and opened it.

'I'd like you to leave,' she said.

'Evie, please—'

She shook her head.

'This isn't what I want.' Her voice was absolutely resolute. 'I've had years of being denied, of feeling like I'm not good enough. I'm not doing this any more.'

The urge to try and talk her round, to make her understand that this wasn't about her, made him hesitate. The pain in her face made him go. With him, it seemed, getting hurt was inevitable. The only good thing he could do here was save her any more of that.

CHAPTER TWELVE

THERE WAS STILL the TV show. She could still get back her old life.

She could pitch up at Purple Productions and with Chester talking the talk she was ninety-nine per cent certain that she could still secure a contract for Season Two of *Miss Knightsbridge*. Her life would be back to the way it was, almost as if the whole Jack Trent mobile-phone-tape scandal had never happened at all.

She even got as far as debating what outfit to wear in order to channel Knightsbridge party girl with a bit more maturity. A lot had happened since the last season. Reality bit as she stood in front of the full-length mirror in the corner of her bedroom, holding up a girly peach dress against her in one hand and wondering if it held its own against the I-know-my-own-mind sharply cut black suit she held in the other.

She really thought the black suit had it. And what the hell was she doing?

The churning in her stomach, so easy to dismiss as the general misery she'd become accustomed to since things had ended with Jack, was actually something more today. A sense of uneasiness mingled with the sadness and anger and she finally faced facts.

Signing for *Miss Knightsbridge* again just felt plain

wrong. Committing to another six months of being someone else instead of being true to who she really was. She'd spent so long doing all she could to seek the approval of others and, really, what the hell had it got her? Nothing but trouble. Nothing but misery. No wonder she never felt secure because she never valued herself, always judging herself by what everyone else thought of her, accepting their criticism at face value.

Enough was enough.

She tossed both outfits on the bed and headed back to the sitting room, pulling out all the paperwork for the jewellery line. The whole project was tied into the *Miss K* name.

There must be some way she could get out of that.

Another weekend of running courses and he really ought to feel more positive about it than this.

The roll-out of the kids' courses had been a huge success. Fully booked within a few weeks of the airing of *Survival Camp Meets Miss Knightsbridge*, and so many enquiries continued to roll in that his admin team were holding a waiting list. He couldn't help referring back to the comment from Evie's insane PR right back at the start of all this. *No publicity is bad publicity.* The press interest in his are-they-or-aren't-they? relationship with Evie seemed to have increased his appeal, and never mind the fact that he'd refused to so much as comment on any of the stories.

He shoved that thought away. Left undiverted, his mind kept drifting towards her at a moment's notice. To counteract that, he'd upped his contact with Helen, her progress and well-being always on his mind, only to find that she was increasingly hard to get hold of. When he did track her down she was always on her way to college, or out to meet friends, or looking into this or that job opportunity. With sudden clarity he saw that he'd been so wrapped up in his own guilt at letting her down that he'd failed to see she'd moved on long ago. He was still in the same place, still beating himself up, still trying to make up for the past. Four years down the line he felt more directionless than ever.

He lay back on the Highlands hotel single bed and pointed the remote control at the tiny television. Down in the bar he had no doubt that his team were in full-on swing with snacks and drinks. Sunday evening, weekend courses done and dusted, the full contingent of children taking part having departed that afternoon after loving every moment of the course he'd run.

It was all a bit too déjà vu for him here now. Same hotel room. Same tasks. Camping out in the forest with all the survival demonstrations. No Evie along any more. The success felt vaguely hollow without her. She'd made his successes feel all the more worthwhile. She'd made him feel better about himself than he'd felt in years.

The news headlines finished and his stomach performed a miserable lurch. Unmistakeable. The groovy über-hip title music for none other than *Miss Knightsbridge*. The brand-new series. Payback for all that hard publicity work Evie had put in. He pressed the button to switch channels and nothing happened. Great—was there anything in this hotel that actually worked? He smacked the remote control against his palm and pressed random buttons madly. Nothing. He swung off the bed and headed over to the TV set to switch channels manually. The screen showed a glossy bar in Knightsbridge as his finger hovered over the off switch.

Why the hell was he torturing himself? He did not wish to be reminded of his monumental mistake yet part of him couldn't help wanting a glimpse of her. Possibly in the hope that she wouldn't be as utterly gorgeous as his memory insisted she was. Perhaps if he could see she really wasn't all that it might help him to finally get over this.

Minutes passed. His hand returned to his side and he sat down on the end of the bed. All the way to the first ad break he watched. She was the star of the show—right? The central character. So why were the rest of the moronic bunch there but not her? It became gradually clear that a skinny girl with a cut-glass accent and a sheet of dark hair, which she kept tossing back, was the central character. She was in every scene, the camera practically winking at her.

What the hell? Where was Evie?

He picked up his mobile phone, angry with himself for his curiosity, which told him he was nowhere near close to moving on. The PR manager at Purple Productions was delighted to hear from him.

'Jack! Darling! Just the person—it's so good to hear from you! Have you spoken to your agent about renewing your contract? We're thinking a select few more *Survival Camp Extreme* shows with celebrity guests, capitalising on the success of the *Miss Knightsbridge* tie-in...'

Over his dead body.

'Why is Evie Staverton-Lynch missing from *Miss Knightsbridge*?' he snapped, talking over her as he continued to stare at the TV. 'I'm watching the show right now and there's some bohemian madwoman in the central role. Annabel Something-or-other. Calls everyone "sweetie".'

'You mean Annabel Sutton,' the PR said patiently. 'We increased her role when Evie left. Pity really. The rankings aren't rallying so far. Evie had a more universal appeal. Annabel seems to put people's backs up.'

No shit. His mind screeched to a halt.

'Evie left? You sacked her after all? Even after she did the survival show and it was a success?'

His mind was reeling.

'Chill, darling,' she said soothingly. '*Of course* we didn't sack her. The news that you two were an item was a gift publicity-wise. We were actually hoping *you* might consider guesting on *her* show, get even more crossover with the fans.'

He was speechless for a moment. To appear on *Miss Knightsbridge* he would have to be drugged or dead.

'But then she didn't renew her contract,' she carried on. 'Her choice, not ours. We tried to talk her round, but Evie was having none of it.'

'We're not an item,' he said automatically, his mind working overtime. Hadn't the whole reason for her doing his survival show in the first place been so that she could *keep* her TV contract? Why do it, all the outdoor tasks, only to turn the contract down herself?

'I thought she was going to launch some jewellery shop?' he said, his mind groping for some foothold.

'She was. Such a pain, we'd even filmed her finding the right premises. The brand was a TV tie-in—she'd paid for the rights to use the *Miss Knightsbridge* name. All that's been dropped too now. Jack? *Jack?*'

He clicked the phone off and stared at the TV screen. Annabel was now in a swanky salon having her hair done. What the *hell* was going on?

Chester Smith was all apologies.

'I can't speak for Evie any more, I'm afraid. She no longer uses my services. However, should *you* be in the market for representation...' he tapped Jack in the centre of the chest with one finger and gave him a wink '....look no further.'

'Are you having some kind of a laugh?' Jack snapped.

Chester walked ahead of him into a messy office with a huge glass desk in the middle of it.

'Absolutely not. You're still able to draw effortless column inches.'

'Why does Evie no longer use your services?' Jack cut in.

Chester sat down, leaned back in his chair and fiddled with a gaudy paperweight.

'She's decided to bow out of the public eye. Something about not wanting to trade on the Staverton-Lynch name.' He threw an incredulous hand up. 'Thing is, Jack, without the name and the glossy lifestyle, who the hell is she? The public don't want to watch some nobody living a normal life. Sometimes you might have to fudge reality a little bit but what the hell? The viewing figures speak for themselves. Evie understood that.' He shrugged. 'At least I thought she did.'

She'd sacked Chester Smith? The man who'd masterminded her reality TV career. Bringer of the glossy glamour photograph and the talking-head fashion interviews. Bowing out of the public eye? What the hell was going on here?

The shop was tiny. Not the glossy, candy-pink premises that he'd seen on the Purple Productions website; this was in a side-street, off the beaten track. No sign outside with the *Miss K* logo on it. Instead the painted sign, teal-blue background with a black handwritten font, said Amelia Jewellery. Not a Staverton-Lynch name drop or a TV tie-in in sight. The window was full of jewellery samples, swirls of silver, pendants, rings, carefully displayed.

He went inside.

She was minding the place herself. No minion in charge while she swanned off having her nails done. Instead she stood behind the small counter at the side of the shop, layers of delicate blue tissue paper lying ready for gift-wrapping. The place wasn't exactly mobbed but a couple of female shoppers left as he walked through the door, taking a ribbon-tied bag with them.

Her face froze when she saw him and he ran a hand nervously through his hair.

'Amelia Jewellery?' he said, because he didn't know where to start. Maybe he could somehow gauge his reception through small talk. If that was the case, it didn't bode well. Her voice channelled coldness.

'It was my mother's name,' she said. There was a pause, during which he waited for her to just tell him to leave. When she didn't, the tightness around his heart loosened the tiniest bit. 'I didn't want to trade on the TV show, but then I realised to properly do this on my own I'd have to drop the family name too. Even though I left the show people still recognise Staverton-Lynch. They think they know me.'

The barbed point hung in the air between them.

'Why didn't you tell me you left the show?' he said.

'Would you actually have been interested?' she asked. She held his gaze for a moment questioningly, then seemed to think better of it, dropping her eyes and crossing to a glass display shelf of swirly silver pendants. She moved a few items around, not looking at him.

'Of course I would.'

'I wanted to go it alone for once,' she said. 'Without

hedging my bets by using the *Miss Knightsbridge* name, or any kind of front for that matter.'

'That's great,' he said, meaning it. She'd had so much to be confident about but had never taken that final jump before. It couldn't have been easy to give up her fall-back position.

'Thanks,' she said.

The awkwardness hung between them. He groped for a place to start that wouldn't sound utterly crap.

'I told my father about the shop,' she said conversationally. 'About leaving the TV show.'

'Was he pleased?'

She laughed out loud.

'You'd think! He liked the name of the shop. But in every other way he was exactly the same gruff nightmare that he always is.'

'I'm sorry,' he said.

'Don't be,' she said. 'It was exasperating. After all his complaints about my TV stuff, I stop the show and he still isn't happy. But then I went away and thought it over and I realised that exasperated is a lot better than crushed. A few months ago I'd have been gutted at yet another knockback from him. Now I just feel…resigned. He's not going to change, no matter what I do.' She shrugged. 'Maybe it's the military man in him. I think you were right about that. He's dealt with everything in the same way since my mother died, as if it's an army exercise. Arrangements in place for me and my brother. Every detail taken care of and never mind the affection. He's giving me all he can give. I can respect that.' She paused. 'For my mother I can respect that.'

She moved behind the counter and began unpacking some gift bags from their cellophane binding.

'I realised when we were together, I have to stop letting the past affect everything I do. There I was, preaching to you about that, about not letting decisions you can't change stop you moving forward now, and all the time there I was defining myself by the last twenty-odd years of feeling inadequate.' She laughed a little. 'I need to accept reality. Stop trying to be something I'm not because I'm so desperate to be liked that I'll dance to anyone's tune.'

Bloody hell, she sounded well adjusted. He'd been counting on a bit more missing him and a bit less looking to the future if he was honest.

Did he have any idea how difficult it was to keep a positive expression on her face since he'd just walked through the door as if nothing had happened? It made her cheeks ache and so she retired to the counter to mess about with the gift-bag delivery, just so she wouldn't need to keep looking at him and channelling positivity and happiness when her broken heart was still at the stage of healing where ripping the plaster off would set the wound right the way back to square one. She wasn't going to stand for that. It had taken all the strength she could muster to walk away from what she knew. Her own tried and tested way of feeling as if she wasn't a total failure. Not signing the new contract for *Miss Knightsbridge* had been almost unthinkable, but she'd done it anyway. Somewhere along the way she'd lost sight of her own hopes and dreams in favour of those of her party-girl alter ego, and if she was ever to be happy with who she really was, the alter ego had to go.

'I'm sorry about the breakfast show,' he said. 'Really sorry.'

She drew in a breath.

'So you said at the time,' she said.

'Evie...' he began.

She talked over him loudly, not wanting the explanation, not wanting to be swayed. She'd got her head straight now, she was moving forward, the last thing she needed was him coming here and throwing a wrench into the middle of that.

'Have you any idea what it meant to me to find you?' she asked him. 'To finally find someone who was interested in what I'm really like? In my hopes and dreams instead of all the trappings, the TV image. None of that stuff is real. It was such a relief to be myself that weekend with you, even if it came with mud and horrible food and outdoor living. I kept thinking at any moment you'd back off, you'd realise that actually I'm not all that after all.' A smile touched her lips at the thought. 'I knew you were reluctant to go public but I didn't realise I meant that little, that you'd clearly never planned to go beyond it being our little secret.'

She stacked a pile of flat gift bags beneath the counter, the perfect occupation to stop herself looking at him. If she did that she wasn't sure she could keep channelling that-ship-has-sailed.

'I wish I'd followed my instincts at the start, after the Highlands weekend,' she said. 'Just left it where it belonged, as an ill-judged fling.'

'Don't say that!'

She faced him down.

'It's the truth.'

He stepped towards the counter and seized her hand in his. Her heart, lagging behind her brain, gave a delighted skip at his touch.

'I was afraid to go public with our relationship,' he said. 'It had nothing to do with being ashamed of you. I don't deserve someone as lovely as you. I was scared, Evie, because of the way I've let people down in the past.'

'People?'

'Helen.' He swallowed hard. 'I put myself first, joining up, without a second thought as to what that might mean for her and my mother. By the time I came home the damage was done—it was too late for me to change things for her. The charity work, the kid's stuff, they're all ways of making myself feel better about that, but somehow nothing was ever quite enough. Because when the going got tough, I walked away, no matter what devastation I might be leaving behind.'

'It's past history,' she said gently. 'You can't let yourself be defined by that or you'll never be able to move forward. You'll spend your life paying for something that's done and dusted. And I'm a big girl. If it didn't work between us, then it didn't work, but at least have the balls to properly *try*.'

'I was scared that it did define me,' he said. 'Because my father behaved in exactly the same way. Only ever there when the going was good. Disappearing the second things got difficult. Leaving us to whatever might come. I was scared, Evie. Scared of letting anyone get close to me again in case, somewhere down the line, things got difficult. Would I have that same instinct? To just choose the easy option and leave? I couldn't stand finding out that really was the measure of me after all, so I made sure any relationship stayed casual. With you, it was so obviously more than that, and denying it, keeping it between us, that somehow felt like keeping it nonserious, non-dangerous.' He closed his eyes briefly. 'Of course I was kidding myself. I could keep it as quiet as I wanted—it didn't change the fact that I was falling for you.'

He heard her sharp intake of breath and then her hand crept gently into his. He looked down at it, squeezed her soft fingers.

'You are not your father,' she said. 'You did what he never did. In spades. You came back when you realised what was wrong. You've spent your whole life trying to put things right. You've been there for your family ever since and you've done so much for youth charities and to help kids develop interests and self-esteem so they don't fall into the same rut as Helen. Those are things to be proud of. You've spent all this time making up for what you think was your mess,' she said. 'You need to let it go. Helen has. I read her interview.'

He stared for a moment as his mind processed that piece of information, wondering if he'd heard correctly.

'*Her* interview?'

She nodded.

'She did a really inspiring interview for one of the women's national magazines. All about her experience and how she's come through it with your help. She's hoping to train as a drug counsellor for youngsters. She sounded lovely.'

'She is,' he said shortly. Why the hell had Helen spoken to the press without asking him first?

He checked himself. Clearly because she felt ready and able to, and because she didn't need to live her life with him being overprotective. It had been staring him in the face for ages. Helen was in a good place, looking forward. Maybe it was time he took a step back.

'I've got a copy of the article back at my flat.' She paused as if debating whether asking him to drop by was a good idea and obviously decided it wasn't. 'I'll post it on to you,' she said.

His mind was so reeling with the revelation that Helen had gone public that for a moment he didn't register that Evie had crossed the tiny shop floor and opened the door. He realised she was waiting there, for him to leave, and his heart plummeted.

'Forgive me,' he said.

She threw up a hand.

'What exactly do you want from me, Jack?' she said.

He crossed the room to her and took both her hands in his.

'Nothing,' he said. 'I don't want you to think for a second about what I might or might not want you to be. I want us to give this thing a go, without constraints, without worries about who either of us ought to be and without reference to anyone else.'

She looked up at him.

'None of that counts for anything if it's going to be some kind of dirty secret,' she said. 'If we're going to be together it has to be out in the open, and not because I've forced you into it but because you want it to be like that.'

He tugged his smartphone from his pocket. She stared at him, incredulous.

'You're making a *phone call*? We're in the middle of relationship crisis talks and you're going to *call someone*? The door's over there…'

Her voice trailed away as if she'd lost communication between her brain and her mouth. He was holding up the screen of his phone so she could speed-read.

A comment online…

@SurvivalJackT: Just to confirm the rumours. @evieIT-girl is my girl.

He swiped to the next screen.

A social network update...

Jack Trent changed his status to In A Relationship with Evie Staverton-Lynch.

She somehow managed to regain control over the hinge on her mouth. Her mind reeled as she processed what he'd done, that he wanted to be with her and he didn't care who knew it.

'I wasn't sure I had any chance of persuading you to give it another go with me,' he said. 'I figured I'd just delete them if you kicked my arse out of the door. But they're out there. No secrets. I would have shouted it from the rooftops but I think it'll reach a few more people this way. What do you think? I want to share my life with you.'

He swallowed hard. The social-media thing had been a bit of a gamble but he hadn't known how else to prove he was serious.

She was silent for so long that he couldn't stand it.

'Evie,' he groaned.

She held up a hand.

'There's just one thing.'

'Anything,' he said immediately. 'Anything at all. What is it?'

'The word "share"...' she said.

Her hands crept up either side of his chest and happiness rushed through him. He curled his hands around her waist. They fitted there perfectly. Of course they did. She belonged with him.

'What about it?'

Her face tilted upwards to meet his.

'Just what exactly does *sharing* with you entail? Would I have to eat bugs in this scenario? Or spend time in freezing rivers?'

He smiled.

'Only if you wanted to,' he said.

She narrowed her eyes. His heart stuttered.

'A good answer,' she said, and kissed him.

* * * * *

Mills & Boon® Hardback
November 2014

ROMANCE

A Virgin for His Prize	Lucy Monroe
The Valquez Seduction	Melanie Milburne
Protecting the Desert Princess	Carol Marinelli
One Night with Morelli	Kim Lawrence
To Defy a Sheikh	Maisey Yates
The Russian's Acquisition	Dani Collins
The True King of Dahaar	Tara Pammi
Rebel's Bargain	Annie West
The Million-Dollar Question	Kimberly Lang
Enemies with Benefits	Louisa George
Man vs. Socialite	Charlotte Phillips
Fired by Her Fling	Christy McKellen
The Twelve Dates of Christmas	Susan Meier
At the Chateau for Christmas	Rebecca Winters
A Very Special Holiday Gift	Barbara Hannay
A New Year Marriage Proposal	Kate Hardy
A Little Christmas Magic	Alison Roberts
Christmas with the Maverick Millionaire	Scarlet Wilson

MEDICAL

Playing the Playboy's Sweetheart	Carol Marinelli
Unwrapping Her Italian Doc	Carol Marinelli
A Doctor by Day...	Emily Forbes
Tamed by the Renegade	Emily Forbes

Mills & Boon® Large Print
November 2014

ROMANCE

Christakis's Rebellious Wife	Lynne Graham
At No Man's Command	Melanie Milburne
Carrying the Sheikh's Heir	Lynn Raye Harris
Bound by the Italian's Contract	Janette Kenny
Dante's Unexpected Legacy	Catherine George
A Deal with Demakis	Tara Pammi
The Ultimate Playboy	Maya Blake
Her Irresistible Protector	Michelle Douglas
The Maverick Millionaire	Alison Roberts
The Return of the Rebel	Jennifer Faye
The Tycoon and the Wedding Planner	Kandy Shepherd

HISTORICAL

A Lady of Notoriety	Diane Gaston
The Scarlet Gown	Sarah Mallory
Safe in the Earl's Arms	Liz Tyner
Betrayed, Betrothed and Bedded	Juliet Landon
Castle of the Wolf	Margaret Moore

MEDICAL

200 Harley Street: The Proud Italian	Alison Roberts
200 Harley Street: American Surgeon in London	Lynne Marshall
A Mother's Secret	Scarlet Wilson
Return of Dr Maguire	Judy Campbell
Saving His Little Miracle	Jennifer Taylor
Heatherdale's Shy Nurse	Abigail Gordon

Mills & Boon® Hardback
December 2014

ROMANCE

Taken Over by the Billionaire	Miranda Lee
Christmas in Da Conti's Bed	Sharon Kendrick
His for Revenge	Caitlin Crews
A Rule Worth Breaking	Maggie Cox
What The Greek Wants Most	Maya Blake
The Magnate's Manifesto	Jennifer Hayward
To Claim His Heir by Christmas	Victoria Parker
Heiress's Defiance	Lynn Raye Harris
Nine Month Countdown	Leah Ashton
Bridesmaid with Attitude	Christy McKellen
An Offer She Can't Refuse	Shoma Narayanan
Breaking the Boss's Rules	Nina Milne
Snowbound Surprise for the Billionaire	Michelle Douglas
Christmas Where They Belong	Marion Lennox
Meet Me Under the Mistletoe	Cara Colter
A Diamond in Her Stocking	Kandy Shepherd
Falling for Dr December	Susanne Hampton
Snowbound with the Surgeon	Annie Claydon

MEDICAL

Midwife's Christmas Proposal	Fiona McArthur
Midwife's Mistletoe Baby	Fiona McArthur
A Baby on Her Christmas List	Louisa George
A Family This Christmas	Sue MacKay

Mills & Boon® Large Print
December 2014

ROMANCE

Zarif's Convenient Queen	Lynne Graham
Uncovering Her Nine Month Secret	Jennie Lucas
His Forbidden Diamond	Susan Stephens
Undone by the Sultan's Touch	Caitlin Crews
The Argentinian's Demand	Cathy Williams
Taming the Notorious Sicilian	Michelle Smart
The Ultimate Seduction	Dani Collins
The Rebel and the Heiress	Michelle Douglas
Not Just a Convenient Marriage	Lucy Gordon
A Groom Worth Waiting For	Sophie Pembroke
Crown Prince, Pregnant Bride	Kate Hardy

HISTORICAL

Beguiled by Her Betrayer	Louise Allen
The Rake's Ruined Lady	Mary Brendan
The Viscount's Frozen Heart	Elizabeth Beacon
Mary and the Marquis	Janice Preston
Templar Knight, Forbidden Bride	Lynna Banning

MEDICAL

200 Harley Street: The Soldier Prince	Kate Hardy
200 Harley Street: The Enigmatic Surgeon	Annie Claydon
A Father for Her Baby	Sue MacKay
The Midwife's Son	Sue MacKay
Back in Her Husband's Arms	Susanne Hampton
Wedding at Sunday Creek	Leah Martyn